A

Diane E. Lindmark

Text and cover copyright © 2018 Diane E. Lindmark

All Rights Reserved

This book or any portion thereof may not be reproduced or used in any manner whatsoever without the express written permission of the publisher except for the use of brief quotations in a book review.

All characters appearing in this work are fictitious. Any resemblance to real persons, living or dead, is purely coincidental.

2023-06

If you enjoyed this book please check out these other books by Diane E. Lindmark

The Stone Family Series

A Solitary Stone Book 1 of the Stone Wall Trilogy
A Stone Falls Book 2 of the Stone Wall Trilogy
The Stone Wall Book 3 of the Stone Wall Trilogy
Heart of Stone Part 1 Passage of Stone
Heart of Stone Part 2 A Stone Divided
The Measure of a Man
Lady Huntsman
Founding Fathers
Hidden Stories

The McLoughlin Family

Safe Haven
Any Port in a Storm
The Eye of the Storm
Storm Bringer
Corruption or Luck

The Crosses

The Christmas Hitchhiker
The Christmas Breakdown
The Christmas Derailment
The Christmas Avalanche
The Christmas Reboot
Dukes and Plumbers
Bjorn in America

Demented Fairy Tales

A Castle Frozen in Time

One Off's

Second Age of Darkness
The Kith
Land and Treachery
One Man's Wife
Legacy
An Accident of Faith
The Wrong Life
For Family Honor
Rough Road

Dedication

I dedicate this, the first of my demented fairytales, to my baby girl Emily on her 12th birthday. I know it is a little dark and a little demented, but I think she is more than mature enough to handle it, and I hope she enjoys reading it as much as I enjoyed writing it.

Happy Birthday Baby Girl

Love, Mommy

Madison

Madison awoke with a start. She rolled on her side and looked at her alarm clock. She reached over and turned it off. She lay there a moment longer, then pushed herself to a sitting position. She had passed a bad night, every bone in her body ached. She scooted closer to the edge of the bed, then slid her left leg out, followed by her right. Her right leg was very stiff this morning. She got up and stumbled slowly to the bathroom. Arriving in front of the sink, she turned on the water and splashed cold water on her face. When she was finished washing her face and brushing her teeth, she opened her medicine cabinet. She groaned as she looked at her morning pill container. She hated it. She sighed again and then popped open Thursday, dumped the pills in her hand, retrieved her cup, filled it with water, and tossed the whole handful in her mouth. She had been taking pills so long she could swallow an entire handful in one gulp. She sighed. This was not something she was proud of, in fact, it was something she was ashamed of, but it seemed like every pill the doctors told her she had to take caused problems, and then they gave her other pills to counteract the problems.

There were times she was really glad her parents had both died, others she missed them, but she did not miss what they did to her when they were alive. They had tried to **FIX HER**. She had never thought she was broken, but they did. She had been born with a deformed right hip socket. Her parents had had it surgically repaired. It had been all right for a while, then it started causing her constant pain, so they had decided that the whole hip had had to be replaced. Then she outgrew the replacement. When she finally stopped growing, they had replaced it again. Now they claimed it would never have to be replaced again unless it wore out, and it again caused her constant pain and discomfort. She had also been born with her right leg being an inch and a quarter shorter than her left, and for one horrible year her parents had tried bone extensions. Fortunately, the doctors determined that her bones were not strong enough and they had had to stop, but that caused its own lingering pain. Her parents decided she needed therapy because she was not a happy child, this of course was its own special kind of torture. Finally, by the time she was sixteen, she had decided she could not take any more and she had tried to slit her wrists. Well technically, she succeeded in slitting her wrists, she just did not succeed in killing herself; which in the end she was rather grateful for.

However, now here she was at twenty years old and still had to have her brother check in on her every day by phone and physically once a week, which in the end made Friday her favorite and least favorite day of the week. She loved her brother, she just hated the fact that he felt he had to check up on her and count her pills. It did not seem to matter how many times she assured him she was never going to try to kill herself again, he was constantly afraid of her overdosing. She sighed again and looked at her watch. If she did not hurry, she was going to be late for work and she could not afford to lose another job. Not that she actually needed the job, but it gave her something to do. Her parents had died and left her and her brother extremely comfortable, neither one of them had to work, but again, her parents had left her brother her guardian, she could not touch a penny of her inheritance without his say so. Not that he was mean about it, but he did watch her and that she hated too.

When she was dressed, she locked up, and headed for the subway. To her relief, she arrived at work ten minutes early. She was just putting her stuff in the locker room when Debbie stuck her head in and hissed, "Whatever you do, don't make him mad today. Ben is on the warpath."

Madison sighed. That was the last thing she needed. Ben was her supervisor and an asshole. He had protested having her put on his team. He said that she would slow down production. She had wanted to protest that this was discrimination. Though she had a limp, she was actually their fastest assembler, and it was not like they were assembling cars. They assembled furniture for customers who had ordered it preassembled, then boxed it, and shipped it to stores for the customer to pick up. She took a deep breath and prayed that God would deliver her from her miserable life. This had been her prayer for the past twelve years. It had not worked yet, but she still had faith. She also firmly believed that God helps those who help themselves, so she continued to help herself.

Charles

Charles was not at all happy about this. He had not been supposed to go on this trip. He was one of the senior programmers. Greg had been supposed to go, but Greg, being the little weasel that he was, had called in sick on Friday morning; then shortly after lunch he had called HR, not his supervisor but HR, and claimed that he was too sick to travel. So upper management had decided late Friday afternoon that Charles would just have to go in Greg's place. He hated this kind of thing; actually, there was not anything about this trip that he liked. He hated team building exercises. He felt that they never did anything to actually build the team, they generally caused friction. He hated the great outdoors. He hated walking. He hated hiking. He had become a computer programmer for a reason. He liked the indoors. He liked his creature comforts. Roughing it was not his idea of fun, not to mention this was going to cause him to miss his son's last basketball game of the year. And since some genius had decided that they needed to get away from civilization, when they arrived at their destination, they were all going to be forced to hand over their cell phones, laptops, and basically anything that required power, which threw his entire life into disarray. He had been forced to take business trips before, but he had always been able to stay in touch with his family. This would be the first time that he would not be able to tell his children good night. This would be the first time that he had not spoken to his wife for a whole day since they had been married, worse than that, it was for five days straight. He was not happy about this, and it caused other difficulties. He shook his head. He did not want to think about it. The work ramifications alone made his head spin. They were already behind on several projects and without him there to supervise, they were only going to fall more behind. He groaned and rubbed his face.

Barbara wrapped her arms around his waist and gave him a kiss on the cheek. "Don't worry, everything will be fine. I'll take care of everything and it's only five days. I'll pick you up on Friday."

He hugged her tightly. "I know. I just have a bad feeling about this trip. Everything seems to be going wrong at the same time."

She kissed him again. "Well then, sir, I think you need to change your outlook on it. Say everything is going to be fine."

He could not help it. He smiled. Barbara was the eternal optimist. It was one of the reasons they worked so well together, they balanced each other beautifully. In so many ways, they were in line. They very rarely argued about anything. Their opinions on everything from religion to politics differed only slightly, but she was the eternal optimist and the outgoing one. He considered himself a realist and was reserved, but he had had to learn young that life was full of hard knocks. Barbara's life had not been exactly easy, but she had managed to remain bright and cheery. She at least came from a warm and loving home with supportive and encouraging parents. His parents were monsters, and he could not ever remember a time in his life where he had liked them, let alone loved them, and they had certainly not loved their children. Their children were merely status symbols. He grumbled, then said somewhat reluctantly, "I will try to have a more positive outlook on this awful business trip."

She sighed and shook her head. "What if I offered you a present on your return if you do?"

He pursed his lips together, stopped, and looked at her skeptically. After a minute he asked, "What kind of present are we talking about?"

She shrugged her shoulders. "I don't know, maybe something silky."

He grinned. "This is going to be the best business trip ever."

She shook her head at him. "I can do without sarcasm, Mister."

Mathias

Mathias sat trying desperately to ignore his mother, who had been droning on and on for well over an hour, she was listing every eligible female of suitable family. He found every one of them to be beneath him, not one of them roused his desire and he certainly could not bear the thought of spending the rest of his life looking at them across the dinner table. Any woman he married had to be worthy of him. She may not be able to be his equal in birth and breeding, but she had better be his equal in appearance. He could not have a woman on his arm that other men found wanting. His mother snapped with irritation, "Mathias, are you even paying attention to me?"

"No, Mother, because we have gone over these women time and time again. I do not care who their father is, or who their grandfather was. That does not change the fact that they are ugly. There is really no other word for it, Mother, and I refuse to marry a woman who is inferior. If she is not a beauty, if every woman does not desire to scratch her eyes out, if every man is not green with envy and wishes her on his arm, I will not marry her. Her teeth must be perfect, her eyes, her hair, her dress, her demeanor, I will not settle for less than perfect, so I suggest you not bring this same list to me again. Find a new list."

Rosemary crumpled the list in her hand. She began clenching and unclenching her fingers, caring not for the paper that had now fallen to the floor, then she glared at her oldest son. "Mathias, you must marry a woman of suitable family."

"What care I for her family? I only care what she looks like in the nude, Mother, and if you expect me to produce those copious amounts of grandsons that you desire, she had better be appealing to me, otherwise you can forget about it. On this I am immovable, so I suggest you had better change your tune."

"You cannot marry just any woman."

"Why not? Father married you."

She grabbed a vase and was about to hurl it, when Jared said, "Mother, control yourself. You talk about birth and breeding, and yet you are the one behaving like an ill-mannered peasant. Do not permit Mathias to provoke you."

She sighed and set the vase down. She smiled at her youngest son. He was her little darling. He had inherited none of his father's looks or demeanor, unlike Mathias, who was every inch his father. She had loathed the man. He had been a barbarian who took what he wanted without care or concern for anyone's feelings. He had kidnapped her and held her prisoner until she was three months gone with Mathias and her father had had no choice but to agree to their marriage. She took a deep breath and let it out slowly. "Very well, I will try to find a young woman who will please us both. Beyond appearance, what do you require?"

He considered for a moment. "The ability to hold her tongue and leave me in peace. Other than her looks and the ability to please me in bed, I really do not care, Mother."

Jared desperately wanted to hit his brother. He delighted in saying anything he could think of that outraged their mother. On one hand Jared understood this. On the other, he would appreciate it if Mathias would be a little bit less of an ass. He decided before another war broke out he should change the subject. "Mathias, what do you intend to do about the wolves that have been attacking the farm animals?"

Mathias shifted in his seat and looked at his brother. He smiled broadly. "I thought you and I would take a bow out the next few nights and see what we can catch."

I

Big Bend National Park, Texas, February 14

Charles was in an especially bad humor. This was the first St. Valentine's Day he had ever missed with Barbara since they had started dating seventeen years ago, and as though that was not bad enough, the weather had been uncooperative. Though he had been told several times that was normal for Texas, he was really starting to hate Texas. He kept telling himself he should not blame the state, it was not Texas, it was the stupid company's fault for deciding they needed team building exercises, and then to decide that what they really needed was inter-team cooperation; so they took members from each of their six different departments – paper pushers, artists, engineers, programmers, advertising, and sales – and threw them together. These were personalities that did not mix. Add this to the fact that none of them wanted to be here, plus of course, the people whose brilliant idea this was were too busy to attend. It made him feel as though he was sitting on a powder keg and somebody had lit the fuse.

The past two days had been the worst in his life. He was sure Barbara would tell him he was being melodramatic, but it truly was. Well, almost the worst. He could think of two separate incidences that were actually worse, but he did not want to think about them. In fact, he wanted to forget that they had ever existed. He nodded to himself. Yes, it was much better to think that this was truly the worst time of his life. He decided to dwell on what made this so much worse. He hated camping, he hated fishing, he did not like the people he was with, and he hated the rain, the wind, the fog, and the cold. Yes, Texas had really shown its ugly side to him. His internal complaining was brought to a halt by Lucy saying with irritation, "Will someone please explain to me why we can't just go home?"

DeVaughn replied with irritation, "Because this is a mandatory work outing and if we don't stay and tough it out, we're all going to get bad scores on our yearly company eval and someone from her department ..." He pointed at Margaret as he continued "... is going to decide that we're uncooperative and the next time there are budget cuts, we'll all get the ax."

Margaret replied with irritation, "Why do you have to bring my department into it? It's your department that has held up our last three projects. Artists are so unpredictable."

DeVaughn got to his feet and shouted back, "I'd rather be an unpredictable artist than a stuck up paper pushing ..."

Charles got to his feet and let out a loud whistle. "Look, nobody wants to be here. We're supposed to be getting along. Remember, teamwork, fair play, all that good jazz, so why don't we stop fighting and try to make the best of this. I'm missing Valentine's Day with my wife to be with you people, so why not make it less miserable for me, and remember our team building coaches are watching and making evaluations. In the end, it's the reports that they send back to the company that actually matter, and right now what those reports are saying about us all is we're a bunch of uncooperative assholes."

DeVaughn sighed with irritation and dropped back into his chair. "You're right. You're right. I'm sorry, I just don't like being cold and wet."

Margaret snapped, "Who does?"

Charles turned and went for a walk before they had a chance to start another fight. Walking past one of their chaperones, she cautioned, "Stick close to the campfire, these cliffs can get pretty treacherous very quickly. You don't want to get lost in the fog. Couple of years back, a guy got lost in the fog and walked right off the edge of the cliff. That's a very long drop."

Charles was tempted to snap that he would almost rather run off of it if it got him away from this bunch of idiots, but he decided that was a tactless remark and said instead, "I'll be careful." He had only intended to stray a little ways away from the camp, but the further he walked, the quieter and the more peaceful he felt. He had no idea how long he had been walking or how far, but it was getting dark quickly. He was just about to decide he should start heading back, when he heard a woman whisper something. He looked around. There was a fog coming in quickly. He shook his head and said to himself, "It must be the fog playing tricks on my mind." He turned to head back to camp, then he started turning slowly in a circle. The fog now completely surrounded him and he had no idea which direction he was facing. He growled and murmured to himself, "Good job, dumbass, you did exactly what you were told not to do. You got lost."

Then he heard it again, a woman whisper. "Charles."

He froze. He had heard stories of men in the fog claiming to have heard voices, but in reality it was just the fog playing tricks on their mind, a noise in the distance, then their brains with the help of their overactive imaginations filled in the rest, and if there was one thing he did not have a shortage of, it was imagination. He asked himself, "What are you supposed to do when you're lost in the fog with no cell phone and no flashlight?" He considered that for a minute, then looked up. Now he could not see the stars either. He guessed he was going to have to just very carefully feel around. He had come uphill, so if he found down, surely he would be headed back to the camp. He started feeling around, taking each step very gingerly. He had no idea how long he had been moving around when he heard it again.

"Charles."

This time, his head jerked to the right. It sounded much closer and he was sure it was coming from that direction. Maybe it was the rest of the group. Maybe they had come looking for him. He started moving in that direction. He had not gone twenty steps when he heard, "Charles, just follow the sound of my voice. You are almost there, just a little further." He kept walking, certain he was headed downhill, then he stepped out in to thin air. He screamed as he stumbled forward, and then he was falling. The last thing he heard was the sound of fabric ripping.

II

Charles groaned as he regained consciousness. He squirmed a little. His right leg, right arm, and shoulder were killing him. He shifted a little to his left and tried to get to his left knee. Pushing himself up with his left hand, he shivered, and looked around. He had been lying face first in the snow. He struggled to his feet. His jeans were torn and his right leg was bleeding, he was standing in a frozen forest. Everything was covered in a blanket of snow. He slowly turned around, then he stared. Not a hundred feet ahead of him was a green meadow. He shivered again and slowly staggered towards the meadow. When he got closer, it appeared as though the snow just stopped. He hesitated a moment, then crossed the line. It immediately felt as though he stepped into a warm spring day. He turned back and hesitated a moment, then reached out across the snow. He shivered and pulled his hand back. He looked around again and murmured, "I must've fallen and hit my head really hard." He was in what appeared to be a beautiful valley, but everywhere around the valley was covered in snow and ice. In the center of the valley was a large structure. If he was being fanciful, he would say a Castle. He glanced at his watch, it read '02/14 6:43:29 PM'. He looked back at the Castle. It appeared to be the nearest structure, but it was a long walk away. He glanced at his watch again, then he tapped it. His watch was digital, but the display still read '02/14 6:43:29 PM'. He cocked his head to the side and stared at it. He counted to twenty in his head, the seconds did not change. He did not understand. If his watch had broken or the battery had died, it should not be displaying at all, or the display should appear damaged, but it did not. For whatever reason, the display was frozen on '02/14 6:43:29 PM'. "I really must be dreaming." He stood there considering a moment longer. "Well, if I'm dreaming, I might as well enjoy it."

He headed for the Castle. Every step was agonizing and it was a long walk. When he was about halfway to the Castle, he could see a small village. By the time he arrived at the outskirts of the deserted village, he was dying of thirst. He could not remember the last time he had been this hungry or thirsty. He could not ever remember being hungry in a dream, though he had once had a nightmare about being trapped in the desert and dying of thirst, but that had been when he was working on a Western gunslinger videogame and he had chalked it up to overactive imagination and late night programming. He looked at his watch, it still had not altered. As he walked through the deserted village, he found it incredibly strange. Though he did not see a single person, everything appeared as though they had just stepped away. It was like he had walked back in time, or perhaps he was at one of those Renaissance festivals and all the workers were on break. He remembered his parents taking him to one when he was a boy. That was a really long time ago, at least thirty years, he could not have been more than six or seven. He was starting to get an eerie feeling about this and every bone in his body ached. He could not ever remember hurting this much in a dream, or a dream that had been this detailed or this long. He tentatively reached out and touched one of the stone walls. It felt very real. Everything he had touched had felt real. He was starting to think he was not dreaming, but if he was not dreaming, what was going on? "Maybe somebody in the Castle can tell me."

He shifted and headed for the Castle. Fortunately, the road from the village led straight to the gates. He stood there staring at the closed Castle gates, then he looked back at the village, then back at the gates. "Okay, that's more than a little creepy." The village looked as though every inhabitant had just walked away, whereas the Castle appeared to be covered in a hundred years of wicked looking thorns and vines, and there were places where they even appeared to be destroying the stones. He frowned as he examined them. They appeared to be some variety of bougainvillea, but he seemed to remember always thinking of bougainvillea as a cheery plant, this looked dark and twisted. The thorns were at least two inches long and even the flowers themselves looked sad and few and far between, and they were an unusual shade of orange, he would almost call them a pumpkin orange. He wondered if that was normal for bougainvillea. He looked around and saw a section of wall that had collapsed. Approaching, he stared in surprise. The vines had moved away from the broken stones. He was easily able to climb over them.

He appeared to now be in a garden, though strangely enough, everything inside the Castle walls appeared to be completely untouched, except where the bougainvillea had begun growing. He headed down the gravel path. Occasionally there would be huge sections of garden that appeared beautiful and pristine, and then there would be sections that were torn to pieces by the growing bougainvillea, and there were several places where he was certain there were statues, but again, they were covered in the bougainvillea. He continued walking through the garden heading for the Castle. He came across a toppled over statue that had clearly been choked to death by the bougainvillea. On an impulse, he bent down and began examining it. It appeared to be a statue of a hunter from long ago because he carried a bow and a quiver of arrows. He looked through the broken pieces, but he could not find the head, nor any trace of it. He identified fingers, hands, arms, but no head. He gave a shiver. He found that far creepier than the Castle itself. He shook his head, then pinched his arm hard. It did not work, he was still here. He reluctantly continued down the path. He came to what he was certain was the centerpiece of the garden; a fountain, or at least it appeared to be a fountain, but again, it had been torn to pieces by the bougainvillea. He was starting to think if he had any sense he would run for the hills, where ever that was. But what he needed was information. He needed to know where he was and how to get out of here, which only left the Castle. He turned and stared at it. It appeared to be a falling down wreck, two of the towers had collapsed. He took a deep breath, prayed to God for help, and continued on his way.

When he arrived at what he thought was the back entrance to the Castle, the doors were hanging open. He climbed the steps, which appeared to be untouched and entered the Castle. He stared in astonishment. Everything inside appeared pristine and untouched. He called out tentatively, "Hello, is anyone in here?" There was no answer. He entered and began wandering up and down the corridors, occasionally calling out. There was no response, again just like the village, everything appeared to have just been left. He had been wandering around for what felt like hours when finally he stumbled into what appeared to be a Great Hall. He wished he would have paid more attention in history class, maybe then he would know where he was. He was sure it was something from his memory. Maybe that was it, maybe he was in a coma. Maybe this was all a drug-induced hallucination. He could not stand any longer. He stumbled to the large, comfy looking chair and dropped down on it. It was so nice to sit down and to be comfortable for just a minute. He found he could not keep his eyes open a minute longer, he shut them.

Charles awoke with a start. He looked around. He had no idea what had awoken him, but he knew something had.

A voice shouted angrily, "Are you deaf as well as stupid?"

"No, I'm sorry. I must've fallen asleep. I've been looking for somebody. I did not mean to trespass."

There was a ferocious, low growl, that scared Charles to his very depths, then the angry voice snarled, "I said, that is my chair. Get out of it!"

Charles struggled to his feet, but his body was stiff and sore. He lost his balance, fell, and rolled down the three steps. He hit the hard stone floor and groaned. After a moment, he pushed himself to his knees. "I'm sorry. I'm hurt. I don't even know where I am. Where am I?"

"You are trespassing in my Castle, and you have bled all over the rug and my favorite chair! Do you know how difficult it is to get blood out of upholstery?"

Charles found the prospect of getting to his feet impossible. He shifted onto his bottom and stretched out his injured leg. "I'm sorry, I'm sure it's rather difficult, but where is your Castle?"

He heard a snort, then a growl, and the same voice replied with irritation, "You are no longer in your realm, I would think that would be obvious. How did you get here?"

"What do you mean, I'm not in my realm?"

The voice sighed with exasperation. "What do you call your realm? I presume you live in some kind of country or kingdom, but where does this place reside?"

Charles rubbed his head. "I really must be losing it."

"You have not lost it yet, but if you continue to irritate me, you will. Now, what is your realm called?"

Charles sighed and decided to play along. "Earth, I guess. I'm from America, though some people say it's not America, it's the United States. If you ask me tomato, tomahto."

"Well, you are no longer in this Earth you speak of, you are now in the realm of Sogaius. How did you get here?"

Charles was looking around. The voice was moving, but he could not see him. This was not surprising since to the right and left of the throne, he should have realized this was a Throne Room earlier, and behind were covered in red velvet drapes from floor to ceiling. In front of the throne, only the doorway was not covered in red velvet drapes, so the figure could move around behind the curtain and Charles could not see him. "I don't know. I was in the fog and I just kept hearing a woman call my name, and then she told me I was getting closer and closer, and then I fell off a cliff. When I woke up, I was lying face first in the snow. It wasn't even snowing where I was. It practically never snows in Texas."

"Texas. What is this Texas? Is it a village?"

Charles sighed. Somebody was definitely pulling his leg. This was all an elaborate trick. He must be on Candid Camera or something. "It's called a state, but it's more like the size of a country."

Charles paused, when he heard another voice, this one a woman whispering. "Your Majesty, I know it is not my place to tell you what to do, but if he is not of our realm, should we not send him back where he came from?"

"Send him back? You must be insane. He was brought here for a reason, and until I know what that reason is, he stays."

Charles pushed himself to his feet. He shouted angrily, "No, you cannot keep me a prisoner! I have a family! I have to get back to them! Please, if you can send me back, send me back! I'm of no use to you! I know nothing!"

"Please, Your Majesty, let me fix him and then send him on his way. It is not right to tie another to our fate."

"Do not presume to question me, woman! I have spoken and it will be done! He stays, but if it will make you feel better, by all means, fix him, then at least for once you can be of use."

Charles was turning in circles trying to follow the moving voices and the footsteps that sounded like a dog following behind his master. "Please, I beg of you, send me home! I have a wife, children, they need me! I didn't even get to say goodbye." The footsteps stopped. Realizing he had finally struck a chord, Charles pressed the advantage. "Please, I've been away on work. I haven't spoken to my children in days. Please, send me home." He could hear growling, then he heard what sounded like a dog pacing. "Please have mercy, send me home." Charles heard a low rumbling growl.

After what seemed an eternity, the voice said, "Very well, I will give you a short parole, provided you give me your word you will return. I will send you back to your realm for one week to say your goodbyes and to get your affairs in order, and if at the end of that time you have not returned, I will make you regret the day you crossed me. And remember, I can reach into your realm and cause much trouble, so do not cross me. I think I am being excessively generous permitting you to return for one week. Do not push me. Empty your pouches."

The statement so caught Charles off guard, he did not even argue. He quickly emptied his pockets on to a low table. When he pulled out the stone pendant he had found while hiking in Big Bend, he heard a roar of laughter. "What's so funny?"

"That is how you entered our realm. You found one of the witch's pendants. You already possess the key to travel back to this realm. You said you fell off a cliff, that must be how you activated it, a long fall. When you are ready to return to this realm, simply leap from some high point, but I warn you, if it is not high enough, it will not work. I would not recommend anything under two hundred feet, and you had better be back in this room before that clock strikes midnight seven days from now."

A moment later Charles heard a door slam. "What if I don't agree to return?"

He nearly jumped out of his skin when he heard the female's voice right next to him. "He will hold true to his promise. I would not cross him." He turned in a quick circle. She was nowhere in sight.

"Where are you?"

"I am standing right next to you, but you cannot see me because your mind is shut. Apparently, your realm has forgotten to believe in magic."

He waved his arms back and forth, but he neither saw, nor felt anything. "Magic doesn't exist, just something little children believe in."

She sighed. "If magic does not exist, then how are you here, and why has your leg stopped bleeding?"

He looked down quickly. Though his jeans were still covered in blood, there was no wound on his leg, and it did not hurt anymore. A moment later, he felt a strange tingling in his shoulder, then his arm did not hurt anymore. "How on Earth?"

"Were you not listening? This is not Earth."

Charles rubbed his face. "I was listening. I'm just finding this all very hard to swallow."

"Put your things back in your pockets. Do not forget the pendant."

He grudgingly did as she told him to do, though he desperately wanted to leave the pendant behind, then he asked, "How do I get home?" A moment later, a goblet appeared directly in front of him. He demanded, "How can I see that, but I can't see you?"

"Because I am making you see it. Your mind is very narrow, but the amount of effort it would take for me to force you to see me would drain me completely and make it impossible for me to send you home. Take the goblet before you drain me completely and I cannot send you home." He took the goblet quickly. "Now drink it and concentrate on where you were when you left."

"Why don't you send me to my home?"

"Because it takes less energy for me to send you through the door that has already been opened. The medallion is clearly enchanted, which is why it brought you here, but these doors are two-way. Once you travel back, it will shut, but it is still open now and every minute that you argue with me makes this more difficult."

Charles was certain that his subconsciousness was merely trying to wake him up in the hospital in this bizarre fashion, but nevertheless he focused on the last thing he remembered being able to see. He concentrated hard, glad he had a good memory. A moment later, he felt all of the strength leaving his body and right before he lost consciousness, he heard the rustle of fabric.

III

Charles shifted and stirred. He groaned and pushed himself up. He looked around. He seemed to be back on Earth, in fact, it looked like he was lying at the base of Mariscal Canyon, only steps away from the water. It appeared to be early morning. He looked at his watch, it read '02/14 11:22:33 PM', and he watched as the seconds went up one by one. He did not take his eyes off of it until it read eleven twenty-three. He dug around in his pockets, then he found his notebook. Flipping it to a blank page, and wrote down '02/14 6:43:29 PM 02/14 11:22:33 PM'. He was still staring at the written numbers when he heard someone holler, "Charles Brewster?"

He looked around and saw a park ranger heading towards him. He hesitated a moment, then said, "Yes, I'm Charles Brewster."

It took the park ranger a moment to reach his side. "I am Ranger John White. Where have you been? We've been searching for you for almost two days now."

Charles hesitated, feeling confused. He looked around. He decided it was really not a good idea to say anything about his weird dreams. "I'm not sure. I think I must've hit my head. I got lost in the fog and wandered around and I fell. I don't know how I ended up here. I just woke up a minute ago."

John did not believe the man for a minute. No one got lost at the top of the cliff and turned up in the canyon unless they turned up as a corpse, certainly not stumbling around in the fog. He wondered what the guy was on, but said aloud, "Well, I hope you feel up to a long walk. My truck's this way."

Charles replied without hesitation, "As long as I know there's a meal at the other end of this walk, I can do anything."

John started heading for his truck as he asked, "When did you eat last?"

"Last night at the campfire."

John stopped walking and turned around to face the man. "The last time anybody saw you was Tuesday night around the campfire. This is Thursday morning."

He looked at his watch again and tapped it. "But I don't understand. What happened to the missing time?"

John took his wrist and looked at his watch. "Maybe it stopped working and decided to start working again." He pulled a trail bar and a bottle of water out of his jacket pockets and handed it over. "It's not much, but it will get you through until we get back to my truck."

Charles took it gratefully. "Thanks, I feel like I haven't eaten in days."

"Well, if the last time you ate was with your friends, it's been at least thirty-six hours. We'll get you back to my truck and back to the ranger station." John turned and headed for his truck.

Charles chewed in silence. He was starting to think either he really had traveled to another realm, or he was going completely nuts. He did not like the idea of going nuts, so he decided to honestly examine the prospect of having traveled to another realm. He reached into his pocket and wrapped his hand around the pendant squeezing it tightly. It was probably his imagination, but it felt like it was vibrating in his hand. He had the overwhelming urge to hurl it into the water, but before he had a chance to act on it, a cold hand gripped his heart and all he could think about was his wife and children. That horrid, faceless voice had threatened them. He said he could reach into this realm and hurt him, and the woman had warned him not to cross the man. "Six days."

John looked over his shoulder. "I'm sorry, I didn't catch that. Six days, what?"

Charles lied quickly. "Six days since I've been home. I miss my family." *Oh my God, Barbara.* He demanded quickly, "Did anyone tell my wife I was missing?"

"I don't know."

"What time is it?"

John looked at his watch. "Nine thirty-four February sixteenth."

Charles wrote that down. He also again wrote down the current time from his own watch, knowing he would need it later for comparison. It was a long walk back to the truck and by the time they got there, Charles was exhausted. He felt like he had not had a decent night's sleep in days. As soon as they were in the truck moving down the road, he fell fast asleep. He did not wake until John shook him. "We're here."

The next few hours were a blur. He was allowed to call Barbara and let her know he was all right, then he was questioned extensively and subjected to a trip to the hospital for a full physical, including a CT scan, bloodwork, and anything else the doctors decided was necessary from a man who lost thirty-six hours of his life. Somewhere in the middle all of this, he was not sure when, he had been told by his bosses that he was not to come back to work until the twenty-seventh at the earliest. He could take as much time as he needed to recover. When the doctors were finally done, they stood back and scratched their heads and declared they could find nothing wrong with him. He was in excellent health, and despite the amount of blood on his pants, he had no injuries. They were at a loss for words. He had more than a few, but he chose to keep them to himself. The last thing he wanted was a trip to the psych ward, especially when he been promised an airplane ticket home as soon as the doctors cleared him; and since they had no medical reason, they cleared him, and he was taken to the airport and put on the next plane home.

IV

New York City, February 21

Charles could barely maintain his composure. He kept looking at his watch, which was pointless since he had as of yet not corrected the time or the date. He pulled out his phone and looked at the time. Seven thirty, and if he had done all of his calculations correctly it was nine thirty in the other realm, which meant he only had two and a half hours to finish what he needed to do. It seemed to be taking the elevator an eternity to reach the eighth floor. The doors had barely opened enough for him to slip through, before he was charging down the hallway. He knocked frantically on the door.

The door opened and Madison sighed and said sadly, "And here I thought you'd finally decided to trust me. After all, you haven't phoned me in over two weeks, Barbara hasn't phoned me in a week, and no Friday visit." She blinked and stared at her brother. He kept opening his mouth and closing it. That was not like him. He was never at a loss for words. "Charles, what's the matter?"

"I only have a few minutes. We need to talk."

She held the door wide. "Of course, come in." He crossed to the living room, sat down on the edge of the couch, gripped his hands tightly together, started to speak, then shot to his feet, and proceeded to pace up and down. She closed the door and watched him. "Charles, something has you very upset. Did you and Barbara have a fight, or is something the matter with one of the kids?"

"No, everything between Barbara and me is fine and the kids are doing great. Look, I don't know how to explain this. I don't expect you to believe me. I don't believe me! I can't tell Barbara, she'd never believe me. She'd have me in a mental hospital just as fast as she could dial the number."

She crossed her arms over her chest and looked at her brother dubiously. "And since I've been in a mental hospital, you assume I'm more likely to believe you."

He stopped and pointed at her. "Hey, that was not my idea! I tried to come up with other options, but there weren't any!"

She bit back several angry retorts, then said calmly, "I know. What am I not going to believe?"

"Something happened at Big Bend. I found this pendant." He pulled it out of his pocket and held it out. His hand was shaking. "I don't know, it's cursed, magical, something like that. I'm telling you, it transported me to an alternate universe, well, another realm, that was what he kept calling it, a realm. I was there for hours and ... there was this man and this woman there. I don't know what they look like, I couldn't see them. They said I don't believe, that I'm a skeptic. I don't believe in magic. Pretty hard to believe in magic when you've had our life, but you know that better than anybody. Long story short, he agreed to let me come home just to say goodbye, to put my affairs in order. I've done that, I've taken care of everything, everything but you. Look, I know I've been hanging over your shoulder for, you know, the past four years, and I know you hate that, and I'm sorry it's taken me this long to tell you why, but it's because I felt guilty. I should've stopped Mom and Dad. I knew that they were torturing you and I didn't do anything. I failed you. I am your big brother. When I came home and found you lying on the floor bleeding to death, I told God if you came through it alive I would never stop looking after you. I would not let Mom and Dad hurt you anymore. I'd do anything if He would just let you live. I know I'm the one who put you in the hospital, and I know you hated that hospital, but I chose it, and I made sure they wouldn't hurt you, and I checked on you every day, and I'm the one who got you out. It was the only way I could keep Mom and Dad from torturing you anymore. It wasn't the greatest solution to the problem, but it was the best I could do. I should've done better."

Any person who has ever thought about or attempted to take their own life knows a farewell speech when they hear one. Madison said quickly, "Charles, I think you've just been working too much. Maybe, maybe you need a vacation, a real vacation, not a work vacation. Maybe you and Barbara should go away for a couple of weeks. Barbara's parents would love to watch the kids. They love their grandchildren. Look, promise me you're not going to do anything stupid."

Charles put the stone back in his pocket. He crossed to his sister and gripped her face with both hands, he tilted it up. "Madison, I know I sound like a crazy person, but I'm not crazy. I swear to you, everything I said happened and I truly believe that this man will hurt my family if I don't go back. He believes I was brought there for a reason and until he knows why, he wants me back. Hopefully, we'll find out why quickly and I'll come home, but I'm not putting the lives of my family in jeopardy, that includes you. So listen, I'm not gonna be here to make sure you take your medicine and I know you hate it, but it's what's best for you. Every time you try to go off your pills, bad things have happened to you, so please just do what the doctors tell you to do. Go to your appointments, fill your prescriptions, take your pills, and don't give Barbara any shit. I know the two of you don't always get on, and I told her the same thing, though I didn't tell her the part that makes me sound crazy."

She hugged her brother tightly. "So how does it work? How can the pendant take you back there?"

He hugged her and sighed. "According to the angry voice, I activated the pendant when I fell off the cliff. I wish I would've never picked up the damn thing. So he says to activate it, I just have to fall again – a long-distance."

She pulled away and stared at him. "You fell off a cliff?"

"Yes, I fell off of Mariscal Canyon Cliff, so, no small feat, like a thousand feet and lived to tell about it. I woke up two days later lying on the canyon floor right next to the water. Mr. Angry said I need to fall at least two hundred feet."

Madison's mind was racing. She was torn between believing her brother and thinking he was as mad as a hatter. Charles had always been stable, she could not believe that he had suddenly gone crazy. "When you woke up, did you go to the hospital?"

He pushed her to arms reach and gave her a little shake. "Madison, I'm not crazy. Yes, I went to the hospital. They did a full exam, drugs, brain scan, the whole nine yards. I wasn't on anything, I didn't hit my head, there's no brain damage. I didn't have a hallucination, so there's nothing making me act crazy or see things. This happened!"

She hugged him tightly, her mind still racing. A moment later, her cell phone chimed. She looked around and saw the sound was coming from her purse. She crossed to it, picked it up, and returned to her brother's side. She looked up at him. "I love you, and I'm really sorry about this."

Charles looked down at her and demanded, "What?" Too late he saw what his sister had in her hand. Before he had a chance to do anything, she pressed the stun gun to his stomach and sent fifty thousand volts of electricity into him. He fell backwards onto the couch and sat there twitching.

She quickly dug the stone out of his pocket, saying as she did so, "I'm really sorry about that, but it says you will be fine in a few minutes." He groaned and twitched. She hurried out of her apartment, stopping only long enough to lock the door, then she headed for the elevator. Getting on, she hit the ground floor button. As soon as the doors opened, she hit the buttons for every floor except eight, then hurried out of the building. Heading for the street, pausing by the ashtray just outside, she pulled her phone out of her purse and dropped it on top. With any luck, some passerby would pick it up. She knew her brother had a tracking app on her phone. She felt guilty at the idea of giving him the runaround, but she needed time. She hailed a cab. To her relief, one pulled up immediately. She got in and said the name of the first hotel that she could think of that was forty plus stories. Arriving at the hotel, she shoved the cash through the little window and hopped out saying, "Keep the change." She hurried inside and approached the desk, pulling out her ID and bank card.

"Good evening, ma'am. How may we help you?"

Madison smiled and blushed slightly as she said, "I'd like a room for the night with a hot tub and a balcony with a great view, so we can sit on the balcony and have breakfast in the morning."

Karen stared at the pixie in front of her. She could not even be five feet tall. She took the offered ID and card. She examined the picture closely, then she shifted to the date of birth. It said she was twenty, and it was definitely the same woman. The ID said she was four foot nine. She began entering the information in the computer. "Yes ma'am, room thirty-eight sixteen is available. It has a balcony and a hot tub and will give you a fabulous view of the sunrise."

"Perfect, I'll take it." It only took a couple of minutes to have everything filled out.

"Would you like your luggage carried up?"

Madison winked at the woman. "Oh, we don't need luggage." She took the keycard and headed for the elevator. It only took a moment before the doors opened. She stepped on and hit the button for the thirty-eighth floor. It seemed to take forever but finally the doors opened and she stepped off onto the floor. She knew she did not have long. If the transaction showed tonight, it would tell Charles exactly where she was. She walked quickly to her room, inserted the keycard, and yanked it out. The light blinked red. She took a deep breath and tried again. This time it opened. She entered, closed the door, reminding herself not to bolt it, crossed to the phone, picked it up, and hit the button for room service.

"Room service, how may help you?" came the voice on the other end of the line.

"Yes, this is room thirty-eight sixteen. I would like to order coffee, toast, scrambled eggs and bacon for two. Have it delivered about six thirty, please?"

"Yes ma'am, we will have your breakfast delivered then."

Madison hung up the phone and crossed to the little desk. She picked up the hotel stationery. Fortunately, they were not cheap in that department. There were not only full sheets of paper, but envelopes as well. She quickly wrote a letter to Barbara.

'Dear Barbara,

If my body is found splattered on the sidewalk, please believe me, Charles has truly lost it and needs to be put in a mental hospital. He told me that he had been transported to a magical realm by a magic stone and if he did not go back, an evil man was going to hurt all of you, so the only way to stop that from happening was to use the magical stone to transport himself back, and of course, he said the magical stone can only be activated by a fall from a great height. The only way to save his life and stop him from using it was to do it myself, and the fact that I actually believe everything he said just shows how crazy our family is. Please forgive me for any heartache or problems my untimely death causes.

Madison'

She set the letter for Barbara aside, then picked up another piece of paper.

'Charles, if this works as you said it is going to, please forgive me. I will find some way to make the angry man on the other side understand that I had to take your place. I could not allow you to leave your family. I love you so much, big brother. When you speak of me in the future to my niece and nephews, try not to make me sound too crazy.

Yours affectionately,

Madison

P.S. You probably want to tell Barbara everything before she gets my letter.'

She folded the letter for Barbara, placed it in an envelope, sealed it, and addressed it. She was glad her brother and Barbara had lived in the same house for twelve years, she did not have to look up their address, she knew it by heart. The note for Charles she merely folded in half, wrote his name on the outside, and stood it up. If, as her brother said, she disappeared, Charles would arrive here shortly and find the letters. And if her body splattered on the ground in front of the hotel, the police would find them, though they probably would not mail them, but she was confident they would make sure they got where they were supposed to. Nevertheless, she wanted to cover all of her bases. She got a ten dollar bill out of her wallet and placed it with the letter and a note saying.

'Please mail, keep the change.'

She laid everything out neatly, then retrieved the stone from her pocket. Maybe she was as crazy as her brother, but she would swear it was vibrating in her hand. As she crossed to the balcony doors and opened them, she considered what her brother had told her. The stone had probably been in his pocket. She did not like the idea of her holding it as she jumped. What if she dropped it? She stuck it back in her pocket and pushed it all the way to the bottom, then she crossed to the railing and leaned on it. She admired the view for a long moment, then she prayed to God for forgiveness if what she was doing was wrong, but she truly believed what her brother had said. She pulled herself up and hesitated a moment, deciding between her good leg and her bad leg. She decided it would be easier to get her bad leg over first. She looked around to make sure no one was watching. They were not. She swung her bad leg over the railing, followed quickly by her good one. Now she was sitting there perched on the railing. She was sure she was completely mental. She felt not a moment's pause, then she jumped.

V

Charles lay there twitching. He had no idea how long it took him to recover. It felt like an eternity, but it was probably only a minute or two. He pushed himself to his feet and staggered towards the door. It took him a moment of fiddling with the door to get it unlocked. As he exited her apartment, he fiddled with the doorknob lock, his hands seemed to not want to work right. Finally he got it locked. He closed the door and checked to make sure, then he headed for the elevator, cursing the fact that her building only had one. He pushed the down button. The elevator was on the seventh floor, right below him. He cursed as it skipped over him, then he watched as it appeared to stop on every floor. Finally, it came back down to the eighth floor. The doors opened and he stepped on. He pulled out his phone and fiddled with the app that allowed him to check his sister's location. To his relief he was right on top of it, she must be having trouble getting a cab. He stepped off the elevator and zoomed in on the app. She was just right outside the door. Reaching the curb, he looked around. She was nowhere in sight. According to the app, he was only four feet away from her, then he saw the ashtray. He crossed to it and picked up her phone. "Dammit, Madison." He began rubbing his hands up and down his face. "Think, stupid, where would she go? You told her she needed a tall building, what would work?" He hesitated, wracking his brain. "A hotel, the only place that she could have the relative privacy she needs. Why didn't I think of a hotel?" He switched to his banking app and opened her account. He paced up and down in front of her building waiting for something, praying he would get there in time. Finally, a transaction came through from one of the new hotels. He cursed. He knew it was like fifty stories tall. He hailed a cab. He hopped in and gave the address and added, "Please hurry." To his great annoyance it seemed like every light was against them. Finally, he arrived at the hotel. He crammed a one hundred dollar bill through the window, jumped out, and ran inside. He approached the clerk and demanded a little breathlessly, "You just had a woman check-in, about yay tall." He held his hand out."

Karen stared at the man. He was quite good looking and married, that explained the no luggage. She said somewhat cautiously, "I'm sorry sir, we cannot give out guest information."

Charles hesitated, then he said quickly, "No, you don't understand. Madison Brewster, she's my little sister."

Karen asked, "And how old is your little sister?"

Charles felt a little guilty as he said, "Sixteen."

Karen's eyes widened and she looked horrified. "But her state ID said she was twenty."

"I thought hotel clerks were good at spotting fake IDs."

Karen was feeling more uncertain by the minute and the managers had all gone home. She was in charge. The man looked old enough to be her father. She said a little uncertainly, "You don't look like her brother."

"Oh, for heaven sakes, we're twenty-two years apart, what do you expect?" Charles grimaced as he realized that math was all wrong, but he did not care, not if it saved Madison. He did not know why, but he felt very certain the angry voice was some kind of dark, horrible monster. He was going to be very angry that Madison was there instead of himself. He could not let her go in his stead, he had to save her.

Karen grabbed her master keycard as she walked out from behind the desk. She said, "David, I'll be on the thirty-eighth floor if anyone needs me. I'll be right back." She headed for the elevator saying, "If you'll follow me, we'll get this sorted out."

Charles most happily followed her. He could not stand still. He kept looking at his watch even though it was pointless. He went over his muddled calculations again in his head. If he had been back for four hours when he had woken up, and he remembered correctly that the Castle clock had read five thirty, and you add the time change from New York to Texas, he did not have much time left, only about an hour but then again none of this made sense, so why would the time make sense? Plus, maybe there was some kind of travel delay. He groaned and rubbed his face. A person could go insane trying to figure this out. When the elevator stopped, he slipped out as the doors were opening and demanded, "What room?"

"Thirty-eight sixteen to your right. Why are you in such a hurry?"

He said truthfully, "Because I'm very afraid my sister's about to do something very stupid."

Karen immediately thought about her request for a room with a view. She hurried towards the door. Arriving, she hesitated only a second before she inserted the keycard and just opened it. She did not care if it was a violation of hotel policy and she got fired. She was not going to let a young girl commit suicide on her watch. As soon as the door was open, the man pushed past her. He shouted, "Madison, please we need to talk! Don't do anything!"

Charles immediately saw that the balcony door was open. He headed for it. He swallowed hard as he crossed to the railing. He looked over. He did not see anything. He looked all the way around the railing, nothing. He felt like falling down crying. She was gone.

Karen's eyes immediately alighted on the envelope sitting on the little desk next to a note.

She crossed to them and picked them up. The note was addressed to Charles Brewster, the envelope Barbara Brewster. When the man re-entered looking shaken, she said, "Are you Charles? Please tell me there wasn't a body out there."

Charles crossed to her and yanked them out of her hand, saying as he did so, "No, she's gone." He crossed to the bed and sat down, staring at his sister's neat handwriting. After a minute he opened it and read. He broke down crying and clutched the note to his chest.

Karen was more than a little confused. If there was not a body, where had she gone? Surely had there been a body, she would have heard about it by now. She asked gently, "Should we call the police?"

Charles pulled himself together and wiped his eyes. He got to his feet. "I'm my sister's legal guardian. I'm going to take her purse with me. If you have a problem with that, call the cops, but since I think the last thing you want is the scandal of a missing teenage girl from your hotel, I suggest you let me go home and report her missing from there."

Karen felt very confused. She asked, "But I don't understand. If she didn't jump off the balcony, where did she go?"

Charles lied quickly. "She was dating a man I didn't approve of. He's thirty if he's a day, clearly far too old for her. They probably ran off together." He got to his feet and gathered up all of her things. "Go ahead and close out the room rental or whatever, check her out. She won't be coming back. Here's the room keys." He handed them to the woman and headed for the door, then went to the elevator. He just kept shaking his head. He had had a week to think about it and he had not thought of a hotel. Madison had planned it all in seconds and knew exactly what she was doing before she ever stuck that damned stun gun to his stomach. He had always thought she was smarter than him, now he just had to pray she was stronger than him and able to survive whatever was going to happen to her. He had to fight back tears as he stepped off the elevator and headed for the street. Arriving, he hailed a taxi, and headed for the train station and home.

VI

Mathias paced up and down his Throne Room. Every time he turned his back on his throne, he glanced up at the clock. That wretched man was now three quarters of an hour late. He really hoped he was not going to be put to the trouble of following through with his threat. He paced for a few more minutes, then all of a sudden the hair on the back of his neck stood up. He moved swiftly out of the Castle. By the time he hit the grounds, he was at a full run. He began sniffing, turning his head from side to side. He shifted his direction. The tingling on the back of his neck was getting worse, and the smell was too. He strained as he ran as fast as he could. He could not remember the last time he had really stretched his legs. Nearing the river that ran along his Western border, he heard a scream. He shifted directions. Fortunately, his night vision was excellent. He saw someone in the water, struggling, then he saw them go under. This section of the river was not particularly dangerous, but it became more treacherous a few hundred yards downstream. He did not break stride as he headed for the bank, dove, and hit the icy water. Fortunately he knew every inch of this river like the back of his hand. He came up a minute or two later, his arm wrapped around someone. He swam to the bank, struggling against the current. Luckily, whoever it was was small and light, he easily threw them out of the water as the current pushed him downstream, then he was able to grab onto the bank and jump out himself, only twenty or so yards further downstream. He frantically shook the water from his hair as he headed back to the woman, at least he guessed it was a woman, who was lying immobile in the snow. He turned her on her side and patted her on the back several times. After a minute she coughed and sputtered but did not wake. He pressed his ear to her chest. He could hear her breathing. He growled, picked her up, and slung her over his shoulder, and hurried back to the Castle. Arriving, he headed for the guest wing, entered one of the guest rooms, gestured to the fire and it immediately sparked, then began glowing. By the time he laid her on the floor in front of the fire, it was burning brightly. He touched her cheek. She was freezing to the touch. He stripped her out of her wet clothes and bellowed, "Someone bring me some towels."

Gretchen appeared at his side a moment later, a stack of towels in hand. He yanked one of them off and began drying the girl. He was having a hard time determining whether she was a woman or child. As he began drying her hair, he saw blood running from a cut. He ordered, "Fetch Louisa."

Gretchen curtsied. "Right away, Your Majesty."

He folded the towel, slid it beneath her head, then he shifted her head and laid the bleeding side down on the towel. He picked up another towel from where Gretchen had placed them and went back to drying the rest of her body. He leaned in and smelled her neck. She smelled disgusting. The smell was so strong it almost made him gag. He continued drying down her body. He smelled between her small breasts. He snorted and fought to not sneeze. He looked away. He moved down from her waist to her hips. In the firelight, he saw a long disfiguring scar that ran from an inch or two above her right hip down about seven or eight inches. As he moved the towel towards her knees, he leaned in and smelled the scar. He could smell something unnatural beneath the surface. He sniffed several times, then he tentatively licked the scar, sputtered, and spit. He shook his head and his shoulders as he tried to get rid of the taste, he thought licking the fireplace would taste less disgusting. He moved further down, then he saw on her right calf several circular scars about the size of his thumb. They seemed evenly spaced around her calf. He finished drying off her legs and leaned in and smelled the scars.

Louisa asked, "What does your nose tell you?" He snorted, sneezed, then shook his head and shoulders several times. Louisa gave a little screech as water droplets flew everywhere. She picked up a towel and threw it over him. She said with irritation, "You smell like wet dog."

He snarled and snapped, "I see you are still cross with me."

"It was wrong of you to demand that man return."

"Well, right now you have bigger problems to deal with. This ... whatever she is, is bleeding." He gestured to the creature in question.

"Why do you say whatever? She appears to be a young woman."

He snorted and shook his head as he gripped the towel and began drying off. "She does not smell like a woman. She smells unnatural and disgusting."

Louisa carefully walked around the girl and knelt down. She turned her head over and began examining the wound. It needed to be cleaned. "I am going to need more light. Can you bring me a lamp?"

Mathias snorted and said with annoyance, "You choose the most inconvenient times to choose to do something the mundane way."

She looked at him innocently and blinked. "I have no idea what you are talking about, Your Majesty."

"You did not require anything to treat his wounds, yet now you require a lamp to look after her." He exited the room and returned with the lamp and turned it all the way up. He ran the lamp over her body. He shook his head and demanded, "What did they do to her?"

Louisa applied pressure to the head wound, then followed his gaze. She stared at the scars and slowly shook her head. "I have no idea. I have never seen wounds like that." She cocked her head to the side, then tentatively ran a finger along the scar at her hip. "This one has been cut open many times. I do not understand, that makes no sense." She looked up at him in confusion and shrugged her shoulders, then she looked back at the girl. "But it is obvious her soul has been tortured. She is wounded, bowed, and beaten," she looked back at him, "but not broken. Get a blanket. It is not right for her to be lying here naked in front of you."

He snorted and shrugged his shoulders. "Why? She is but a child. She does not appeal to me in the least." Nevertheless, he stepped away and returned with a blanket and covered her with it.

Louisa snorted with amusement. "That shows what you know, she is a woman fully grown."

Mathias leaned in and sniffed several times. "She does not smell like a woman. What is wrong with her?"

Again she shrugged her shoulders and returned to cleaning the wound. When she felt confident it was completely clean, she carefully began pinching it shut. It only took her a few minutes before the wound was closed without a trace of a scar. "I do not know, but she is not from our realm, so who knows what they did to her there."

Mathias picked up her clothes and began examining them. He had never seen anything like them. He stared at the strange corset. It had taken him a minute or two to get it off. He turned it over in his hands, then he picked up her strange tunic and examined it, finally her britches. She had had no shoes on, they had probably been lost in the river. He noticed there was an unusual weight to one side. He remembered that the man had had pockets in his pants. After a moment of feeling around, he discovered some hidden pockets. He stuck his hand in and pulled out the pendant and cursed. "Unbelievable, that wretched coward has sent this girl in his stead."

Louisa looked up from what she was doing. "What do you mean?"

He held the pendant in front of her. She gave a little gasp, then looked down at the girl and back up at the pendant. "He did not strike me as a coward, but I must say it is curious how she ended up with it. Maybe she stole it from him."

Mathias snorted with amusement. "She is not even five feet tall and does not even weigh seven stone. He was well over six feet tall and must have weighed at least fifteen stone, he probably tricked her into taking it, then threw her off a cliff." He squeezed the pendant so tightly for a moment he thought he was going to break it. There is nothing in this world he hated more than someone who preyed on the weak and helpless, and whatever this thing in front of him was, woman or child, she was clearly incapable of looking after herself. He would have to find a way to teach that little coward a lesson.

Louisa frowned. The man she had spoken with clearly cared about his family. She found it impossible to believe that he would have tricked this girl. She sighed and gently caressed the girl's cheek, saying softly as she did, "Rest, regain your strength." After another minute of gently rubbing, she looked over her shoulder again. "She will sleep till morning, but her hair is covered in blood. I will go and begin filling the bath. Will you help me get her in it?"

He crossed his arms over his chest and said with irritation, "I thought she should not be naked in front of me and now you want me to help you bathe her?"

She got to her feet. "I said get her in the bath, I did not say bathe her, and since you have already seen her naked, it seems preferable to have you assist me than two of the footmen."

"She is the size of a child. If one of my footmen could not handle her, I would dismiss him on the spot were that something I was capable of doing, but yes, I will help you."

An hour later, Mathias laid her in the bed, trying not to breathe through his nose. It was difficult. It was not natural for him to breathe through his mouth. He had hoped the bath would improve her smell, but it had not. Whatever was making her smell so disgusting to him was inside of her, or perhaps it was just her own natural body odor. After all, the rest of the inhabitants of his Castle he could not smell. Maybe he had just forgotten what a woman smelled like. He shuddered. *Perish the thought*. He thought he would rather be dead.

Louisa asked, "What is the matter?"

"I was just wondering why she smells so disgusting."

Louisa replied coldly, "Perhaps it is your unnatural distaste for anything that is not perfect."

He snorted. "She is definitely far from perfect. If you do not need me further, good night." Not waiting for a reply, he turned and exited the room.

Louisa was surprised he did not slam the door. His mood had been getting worse since the third tower started to look as though it was going to fall. She ran her hands up and down her face, then she looked down at their guest. She crossed her arms over her chest and said, "And what am I supposed to do with you?"

VII

Madison shifted and stirred. She could not remember the last time she hurt this much, but more than that, she just felt weird. Her room was dark and smelled funny. One of her neighbors must be cooking something weird, hopefully not drugs. Oddly enough, she also thought she smelled wood-burning. It reminded her of when they would have barbecues at the mental hospital. She shuddered. That was not a pleasant memory. She would try not to think about it. She brought her watch in front of her face and pressed the button for it to light up. She blinked and stared at it, the hands indicated 10:16:18, the date said the twenty-first. She tapped her watch, the secondhand was not moving. Her eyes widened as she remembered her conversation with her brother. She lifted her head off the pillow, pushed herself up on her elbow and looked around. She saw a tiny ray of light peeking through a curtain. Across the room she could see a fire burning very low. She started to get out of bed, then she realized she was completely naked. She gasped and pulled the covers up to her chin. She looked around the dark room, she really could see nothing. She had no idea where she was, or how she had gotten here. She listened. She did not hear any noise, nothing, none of the telltale signs that she was in a hospital, noises she was very familiar with, but they were absent, which made sense since she had never been in a hospital with a fireplace. Finally she said softly, "Hello, is anyone here?" There was no response. She reached over and started feeling around. She found a nightstand table, but there was no lamp. She felt the wall, no light switch; then the door opened and the room filled with light as she looked quickly, and saw a woman coming in carrying a tray.

Gretchen said, "Good morning, Madam. Did you sleep well?"

Madison continued to clutch the covers to her chin as she pressed her back against the pillows. She tucked her elbows in trying to make sure she was not showing anything. She said a little hesitantly, "Yes, I think I did. Where am I?"

Gretchen placed the tray on her lap as she replied, "Glacier Guard Castle."

Madison stared at her. "Where is that?" She was not staring so much because of what the woman had said, but at the woman herself. She appeared to be quite translucent. She blinked and continued to stare. She looked like a ghost from medieval times. She wore a long dress, slightly flowing with a short bodice. It was difficult to determine color, but she thought the dress was brown and the bodice was green. She was tall, very slender, and appeared to be about fifty. Again, because of her translucent state it was difficult to determine the color of her hair, though she thought it was a graying blonde with her hair neatly braided. Unfortunately, she could not tell the color of her eyes either. Madison must have hit her head and landed on a balcony below. Yes, that was the only thing that explained it. She was in a coma, then she laughed at herself. *Really smart, Madison, you jump off a balcony because you believed your brother that he was transported to another world, and now you yourself do not believe the evidence of your own eyes. I have to say, that's amongst the most insane things that you've ever done.* She considered herself for a moment, then nodded. She was right, of course, she had truly believed Charles, and now, here in front of her was a quite translucent woman, clearly magical. Charles had said he could not see the woman who had spoken to him because she said he did not believe. Maybe the woman was translucent because she only believed a little. That made sense. Madison nodded, she felt that it made sense.

Her thoughts were interrupted by a loud male irritated voice from the doorway saying, "It is one of the twelve kingdoms of this land. You are of Earth, are you not?"

She tightened her grip on the covers and looked to the doorway. There was no one there. "Yes, the planet I come from is called Earth."

"Planet, not your realm?"

"I don't know what you mean by realm. I mean the planet we live on is called Earth. It's in the galaxy called the Milky Way and you just exhausted my knowledge of astronomy. Well, that's not strictly true, I could tell you some of the names of the other planets, just don't ask me to put them in order."

Mathias did not know why, but he found that incredibly funny. He laughed. "So you have no idea what your realm is called. This realm is called Sogaius. Our land is called the kingdom of Holdstar, and as she said, you are in Glacier Guard. My kingdom gets its name from the glaciers that we are surrounded by. They magically protect us from our enemies. Our planet is called Tonstant. How did you end up in my kingdom?"

Madison found it a little more than disconcerting talking to the angry faceless voice. He was clearly outside, to one side of the door, either being respectful because he knew she had no clothes, or she had no idea why. Something told her respectful never entered his head. She countered with her own question, "Where are my clothes?"

"Your garments were not suitable for a woman of my kingdom. They were taken away. Gretchen will supply you with new garments. This is the only time I will permit you to answer a question with a question. In future, I expect answers. For now, I will leave you. You cannot exit your room until you are properly clothed."

Madison turned to look at the woman who had backed away and was trying to look unobtrusive. She asked, "Are you Gretchen?"

Gretchen curtsied. "Yes, Madam."

She smiled. "Please, just call me Madison."

Gretchen bit the inside of her cheek as she considered. She had no idea what His Majesty intended to do with the woman. For now it was best to assume that she was of importance. She slowly shook her head. "No, Madam, I do not think His Majesty would like that."

Madison laughed and said, "But I am no one of importance."

"That is for His Majesty to decide. I will wait to receive his orders. For now, why not eat your breakfast, Madam, and I will go see what I can do about some clothes."

She sighed and shrugged her shoulders. "Very well, thank you." She lifted the cover off of her breakfast and was relieved to see that it was eggs, ham, and toast. She did not know why, but she expected it to be something unfamiliar. It was also not translucent. She frowned. The Castle, the linens, everything seemed to be solid. Why were not the people? This was all very confusing. She ate her breakfast and sat waiting. At least an hour had passed before Gretchen returned, her arms full of clothes.

"I am afraid I could find nothing that would fit you without alterations." She placed her bundle on the foot of the bed. She picked up the camisole. "Here, why do you not go ahead and put this on?"

Madison frowned but did as she was told. She frowned. It was rather thin and only went to past her knees. She asked a little skeptically, "Isn't it a little thin and short?"

Gretchen frowned. "I would say for a camisole it was a little long, but as I said, I could find nothing that would fit you without alterations, though I see no need to alter the camisole. However, we will have to shorten the overdress, but I thought given your coloring this purple one would suit you very well, and I think this silver bodice will fit you reasonably well and complement the purple."

Gretchen helped Madison into the purple overdress, then had her try on the little bodice. Madison would have called it a lace-up vest that only went to the bottom of her ribs. It, too, was a little big and would have to be adjusted, but Gretchen carefully pinned it to the correct size, then she knelt down and began pinning the hem of the overdress. Madison found it incredibly tedious to have to stand there, balancing on the ball of her right foot so she would not be lopsided while poor Gretchen knelt on the floor and pinned the overdress, but finally this was done and they were able to remove everything except the camisole. "I am sorry I've been so much trouble."

Gretchen smiled. "It is not your fault, Madam. Is it true what they say, you are from another realm? Louisa brought your garments down last night to have them washed. They were most extraordinary looking." She moved back to the foot of the bed and picked up a robe, then returned and helped Madison into it. "I know it is a little long, but it will keep you warm. The Castle can get quite chilly. I shall return with these garments as soon as I have them altered." She went to pick up the garments and then she said, "Oh my word, I completely forgot about slippers. I will not be but a few moments, Madam."

Madison sighed and frowned, wondering what had happened to her sneakers. Maybe she would at least be permitted to wear those. She would have to ask His Majesty. When Gretchen returned, she was holding two small squares of cloth and a piece of charcoal. She knelt down and put one in front of each one of Madison's feet. "Here, Madam, stand on the middle, I will trace your feet and then I will take these to the cobbler and have slippers made for you."

Madison did as she was told, but she said, "There's one problem with that."

Gretchen looked up at her. "Yes, Madam?"

Madison pointed, then stopped standing on the ball of her right foot. Now she listed. "My right leg is like an inch and a quarter shorter than the left."

Gretchen tilted her head to the side. "Oh, my, that is definitely a problem. Well, I will take these to him and have him make you a pair of slippers and ask him what he can do about that." Gretchen finished what she was doing, then retrieved the garments for alteration and left the room.

VIII

Madison plopped on the bed and looked around. She wondered how long she was going to be stuck in this room. She was feeling worse by the minute and after standing for so long, she was in so much pain she wanted to scream. She tried to find a way to lay comfortably, but it was impossible, and she could not seem to lay still either. She had no idea how long had passed when the door opened and a different woman entered. "Good afternoon, how are you feeling? Did you sleep well?"

"I slept well, but I'm not feeling so hot right now."

She curtsied. "Permit me to introduce myself. I am Louisa and if you are cold, we can build up the fire."

Madison stared at her for a moment, then realized what the misunderstanding was. "No, where I'm from that's a way of you saying you're not feeling well, and please call me Madison."

"Oh, I see. Is there something I can do to help? I am the Castle healer."

She frowned. "I don't think so. Something tells me y'all don't have the same kind of medicine."

"You need medicine? Is it for the pain? Does your leg hurt?"

"It does. How did you know?"

"I was here last night after His Majesty brought you in. I fixed your head."

"What was wrong with my head?"

Louisa shrugged her shoulders. "As far as what was wrong with your head, you had a large gash in it, but how you received it, I do not know. I have no idea how you traveled from your realm into ours, so I cannot say if that is how the injury occurred. The man from your realm, he was badly injured too."

Madison was feeling her head. "I don't feel anything on my head."

"Oh you would not. I fixed it."

"You mean like magically?"

Louisa smiled. "Yes, I can use magic to heal fresh wounds and to help with illness."

She smiled. "Well, that definitely makes you superior over our doctors."

"They cannot heal?"

"They don't have magic. They use medicine and surgery to try to help you. It doesn't always work."

Louisa sat on the edge of the bed. "Is that what happened to your hip? They used surgery and it did not work? What is surgery?"

Madison frowned. "Wow. Surgery is where they take you to a room, they call it an operating room. There they give you medicine that puts you out of it, makes you sleep and then they start cutting you open and trying to fix what's wrong with you. When they're done, they sew you up and you go to another room where you wait until you wake up, and then you go to another room where you stay until they tell you can go home, all the time pumping you full of drugs to try to take the pain away. Then depending on what they did to you, you have something called physical therapy, which is supposed to help what they did to you. I shouldn't be so angry and bitter, they do their best and most people they do help. I just always kind of thought they were out to torture me."

"You did not want them to cut you open? I can understand that. I would not want to be cut open either. It sounds like something you do to an enemy, not a friend."

Madison shrugged her shoulders. "It wasn't my idea. My parents, they were trying to fix me. A specialist said he could make my leg longer."

Louisa shuddered. "That does not sound friendly."

Madison considered for a long time. "I think it might have been different had it been my choice, but it wasn't. I never had a say in the matter."

Louisa nodded. "That would make me very angry." She appraised the girl in front of her. She was really not looking well. She was actually looking worse by the minute. "What can I do to help you?"

She shook her head. "I don't think there is anything you can do. The doctors, they had me on all kinds of medicine. Stuff they said you can't just stop taking, and well, I guess I kind of just stopped taking mine since I left it back in my world. I don't know how long I've been here, but my alarm had just gone off to tell me to take my next batch of pills, so I'm probably at least twenty-four hours overdue on some, maybe even more. Some of them I take twice a day, so I'm now down two doses." She hesitated. The last time she had stopped taking some of her mental pills, she had gone kind of mental. She felt out of control and had been screaming at everyone. "I should warn you some of the pills they gave me, they messed with my mind, and now that I'm coming off of them, I could be really weird again. They are supposed to make me happy, but they really just kind of make me numb, and when I'm coming off of them, sometimes I can be angry or crazy, say or do things I would never normally do. Then there's the pain pills, coming off them, that's gonna make me crazy. Granted, all this is providing the fact that I live through it. They say you can't just quit cold turkey on pain medicine, not when you've been on them as long as I have. Or the other stuff, any of it, coming off of it cold can kill you."

Louisa was not liking the sound of this. It was sounding worse and worse by the minute. She asked, "Medicine for your mind to make you happy, but you said it did not make you happy?"

Madison shook her head. "No, it just made me feel numb. Sometimes when my brother would hug me, I wouldn't feel anything. Sometimes I wouldn't be happy or mad to see him. He was just there. I was just there." She started crying. "But please don't lock me away in a crazy hospital. Kill me before you do that." She buried her face in her hands and cried.

Louisa was looked confused. "What is a crazy hospital?"

She started sobbing harder. "I think they used to call them mad houses or asylums."

Louisa nodded. "A place for the insane." She reached over and rubbed the girl's cheek. "But child, you are not insane."

Madison pressed her wrists into her ribs, not wanting the woman to see her scars. She kept telling herself she needed to stop this. She was being hysterical. She needed it to be calm, but she could not seem to help herself. She just sobbed harder.

Louisa's heart was bleeding for the child. She reached over and pulled her into her arms. She pressed her head to her breast and began stroking her hair, murmuring softly, "Be calm, child, let your heart be at peace. There is nothing here to upset you. Be calm …" The sobbing started lessening. "… Be calm, let not your heart be troubled. Rest, find peace. Close your eyes and sleep. No one here will hurt you, sleep, child." She continued repeating these things until she felt Madison go limp in her arms. She held her a little longer, continuing to weave her magic. She wanted to make sure that she was out and would sleep the rest of the day. She would be sure to be here in the morning when the child woke. She clearly could not be left alone right now. Finally, she laid her back against the pillows and covered her with a blanket.

IX

Louisa continued to stare down at the girl. She found this entire thing very disturbing. After another minute she said coldly, "You know, Your Majesty, eavesdropping is quite unbecoming of a gentleman."

Mathias stepped through the wall. "This is my Castle. I make the rules and listen to what I like. There are no secrets from me in my Castle." He hesitated a long minute, then added, "And since when do you accuse me of being a gentleman?"

She sighed and shook her head. "What are you going to do with her?"

Mathias chose to ignore that question, mainly because he had no answer, and he never admitted to his subjects that he did not know something. He felt it was a sign of weakness. Instead he countered with, "Do you understand what is wrong with her? Will you be able to help her?"

"I believe what is wrong with her right now is some form of withdrawal, like when a drunkard quits drinking, but this is very different." She turned to look at him. "You did not answer me last night when I asked you what you smelled. It might help me."

He shrugged his shoulders. "As I said, she does not smell like a woman." He moved closer, inhaling deeply, considering with every breath.

Finally he said, "When someone is a drunk, you know how you can still smell the alcohol even when they are not drinking? It is like they sweat it. I think that is what it is. I do not think it is her I am smelling ... but things inside of her that are changing how she smells." He could see sweat glistening on her face and neck. "If I touch her, will I wake her?"

Louisa smiled. "You could pick her up, throw her over your shoulder, carry her to another room, and throw her on the bed and she would not wake."

He pulled the covers back and licked her neck. He gagged and sputtered. "Yuck, she tastes even worse today than she did last night, and I did not think that was possible."

Louisa was finding it hard not to laugh. She had never seen her King look like this. He looked like he wanted to retch. "Actually, I think that makes sense. The best thing to do with a drunkard is to make them sweat it out. Give them plenty of water and wait for it to pass. I would presume the principle is the same, but something tells me she is going to need a lot more help to get through this." She frowned as she considered. There was not just the withdrawal to deal with, but what was going to happen as weeks and maybe even months went by. Would the girl remain as she was, or would she slowly become part of the Castle? She glanced at the King out of the corner of her eye, and what about him? She had a good sense for when people were telling the truth, and he had definitely been telling the truth last night when he said that she in no way appealed to him, but she did not expect that to last. He was, after all, a man, and Madison was a rather attractive young woman, and unless Louisa was wrong, exactly the kind of woman he would fall for, despite what he thought.

Mathias could see the wheels turning in Louisa's mind. He had told her on many occasions that she had not a poker face and should never play cards. He let her think for a little while, then he interrupted. "But you do think you can help her?"

"Through the withdrawal, yes. I think I can also help with any pain from her leg, but I cannot fix it. You know I cannot fix old wounds, and I cannot help her be at peace with herself. That is something she has to do on her own, all I can do is be a guiding hand."

He huffed and puffed several times as he considered, mulling things over in his mind. Finally he shifted and headed for the door. He tossed over his shoulder, "Do what you can for her, but if she becomes too much trouble, she goes back."

Mathias went to his office and threw himself in his chair. He pulled the witch's pendant out of his pouch and held it up by the cord he had added. He slowly spun the cord between his thumb and forefinger. The pendant twirled in front of his face. *How did you end up in their realm?* he asked himself. *What game are you playing, Witch?* He considered that for several minutes as he watched the pendant twirl back and forth in front of him. *Witches never do anything without a purpose and there are no accidents, only plans other people make that they do not tell you about. Which leads us right back to, what game are you playing, Witch, and who are your players? Who are your players?* He considered the woman in the bed two floors above him. He frowned. *Was she a woman or girl?* That was an interesting question and one he did not have the answer for yet. He found himself split down the middle, and what was he going to do with her? He decided to leave that for the moment and ask himself instead, *Why is she here? Why was the man here? Why now? Why after all this time? What was the purpose in all of this?* He snarled and tossed the pendant in the top drawer of his desk, then he slammed it shut. After a minute he slammed both fists onto his desk and got to his feet, knocking over his chair as he did so. He shouted angrily, "Too many damn questions and not enough answers!" Too late, he realized he had spoken aloud.

Rosemary said quickly, "Questions? I can help with questions."

He snapped, "Shut up, Mother. Nobody was speaking to you."

"If not me, then to whom? There is no one else in the room, just the two of us."

He snarled, growled, then snapped angrily, "I am in the room. You are in a painting."

"But still technically in the room."

He crossed to the painting and yanked the sheet off of it, sending a cloud of dust scattering. He glared at his mother. "Remember what happened the last time you irritated me, Mother. It was seven years before your delightful voice could be heard by anyone. Would you like that to happen again? This time maybe I will scratch out your eyes."

Rosemary took several deep breaths as she glared at her oldest son. She snapped with equal heat, "Oh, how I hate you! I hate you! I hate you! You are a disgusting animal, a murderer, a cold blooded killer whose thirst for blood has put us all where we now find ourselves!"

He pointed to himself and snarled, "Me? You … you blame me for this? I did not do this. I was not the one who created the mess we now find ourselves in. That was you, Mother, and that is exactly why you are trapped in that painting. I, at least, have the freedom to roam the grounds. So tell me who angered the witches more, me or **YOU?!?!**" Not waiting for a reply, he jumped up on the little table and covered the painting with the sheet, then leapt off, landing on all fours. He exited the room, kicking the door shut, effectively silencing his mother.

X

Madison had been up with the sun. Today was the first day since she had arrived where she actually felt like a normal human being. Actually, she felt better than she had felt in a very long time and she was itching to go for a walk and explore the Castle and grounds, but she also wanted to take a bath. She thought she smelled. She had not left this room since she had arrived and she had been so out of it, she was not even sure how long she had been here. She shuddered when she thought about the last few days. She had been kind of a wreck most of the time. She had just been crying and feeling sorry for herself, but there had been a few ugly moments where she seemed to scream at anything and everything. She kept trying to tell herself it was just the medicine, or the lack of it, but she knew without a doubt had Gretchen and Louisa not been here for her, she probably would have either drowned herself or slit her wrists again. That would have been really bad, because she did not want to die, she wanted to live. Her thoughts were interrupted by someone entering. She looked up and smiled.

Gretchen entered carrying a tray. "I brought you your breakfast."

"Thank you. I feel terrible, you've been waiting on me. Tell me where to go and I will get my own breakfast from now on." Madison realized instantly she had said something shocking again.

Gretchen looked stunned and slowly shook her head. "Oh no, Madam, that would not be appropriate. Female visitors to the Castle do not go down for breakfast."

"My apologies, I didn't mean to suggest something shocking. I still think it's terrible to make you wait on me."

"Oh, I do not mind. It gives me something to do. We all think it is rather nice having a visitor."

Madison glanced at her breakfast tray. As always, it looked and smelled wonderful. "I don't suppose it would be possible for me to have a bath before breakfast? I don't remember the last time I bathed, which now that I think about it, is really gross."

Gretchen was pleased to see that the young lady was looking more cheery. Neither she nor Louisa had wanted to suggest her going anywhere near a tub, not when she had been so hysterical on numerous occasions. "Of course, there is the bathing chamber right through here. I will run your bath and then I will fetch your things. What kind of soap would you like?" She headed into the bath chamber. Madison followed her. She stared at the lovely large round bathtub. It was six feet across and appeared to be at least three or four feet deep and there was an edge all the way around for sitting on. Gretchen crossed to the taps and turns them on. "How hot do you like the water?"

"I like to boil."

Gretchen giggled. "Me too."

Madison slipped out of her nightdress and climbed into the tub as she asked, "What are my options for soap?"

"We have rose, lavender, lemon, and honey."

"Lemon, please." She greatly enjoyed her bath and she really enjoyed scrubbing her entire body. She did not know why, but she felt like she was scrubbing the stink of the past few years off of her. She was becoming more optimistic by the minute. Now drug-free, mostly pain free, this was a new start for her, and she intended to make the most of it. She climbed out of the tub and dried off, then she got dressed with Gretchen's help.

"How would you like me to do your hair, Madam?"

"Let me guess, leaving it down would be scandalous."

Gretchen frowned. "A woman should only wear her hair down in front of her husband."

"Then I guess you should arrange it in some manner that will not offend His Majesty."

"Well, I can arrange it very elaborately, or I could just do a simple braid if that is all you wish."

Madison finished brushing her hair and began braiding it. "If a braid is permitted, I can do that myself in a minute." She had scarcely finished speaking before she was done. Gretchen handed her a ribbon and she tied it off.

"And one last thing, Madam, the Cobbler made these for you. He apologizes, but he said with the necessity of making one so much thicker, he does not think such a tiny foot will be able to bend it very well, but it was the best he could do." She held out a pair of small leather boots.

Madison took them and examined them. They were positively the cutest pair of shoes she had ever owned. They were made of soft black leather that went to her knee and on the side of each were six silver buckles that she could adjust for comfort. She slipped her stockinged feet in them and then began buckling them. She held out her feet and examined them. She could not help it, she grinned from ear to ear. "You'll have to introduce me to him so I can tell him how much I appreciate them. These are so cute. I've never had a pair of shoes this cute."

"Of course, I will be pleased to do so."

Madison got to her feet and walked carefully around the room. They were going to take a little getting used to, but every new pair of shoes took some getting used to for her. They were never the same. "Well, other than telling me that I could not leave my room until I was properly attired, His

Majesty did not give me any restrictions. Did he give you any for me?"

Gretchen shook her head. "No, but I am certain he would not wish you to leave the grounds proper, that means do not go outside the wall."

"Will he be angry if I explore the Castle?"

"Not as long as you stay away from the family quarters and his private office."

"And how would I know these?"

"The family corridor is the opposite wing and His Majesty's private office is off the main entry. If you are standing with the main door to your back, there is a corridor to your right. The first two doors to the right are public rooms, the next two rooms on your right are private rooms. I would not go into them, and the only door on the left leads to the Throne Room. Unless summoned there, I would not go there either."

Madison nodded. "That all seems easy enough to remember." She exited her room and went exploring. She had been wandering around the Castle for over an hour when she stumbled upon a corridor blocked by fallen stones. She stared at it in surprise. Everything about the Castle was so meticulously maintained, this struck her as out of character. She cocked her head to the side as she continued to stare at it. She was startled by a voice demanding, "Do you like how I am redecorating the Castle?"

She started and turned around, but there was no one there. After a minute she demanded, "Why do you always speak to me from around corners or outside of rooms?"

"Because I am really not in the mood to hear you scream. Perhaps another day, I might enjoy that, but this is not that day."

Madison was not sure how to reply to that. Everything she thought of, sounded rude. After a moment she said, "Are you afraid you'll scare me or disgust me?"

Mathias snapped back, "I am not afraid, but I know I will scare you, and you will scream, and I do not want to hear it."

"You'll find I do not scare so easily, and I did want to thank you for your hospitality. I know you didn't want me here. Perhaps we should discuss what you want to do with me now, but it's very difficult talking to someone you can't see."

He snarled. "Very well, but if you scream, I swear I will throw you back in the river where I found you." He took a deep breath, then stepped around the corner prepared to plug his ears. To his surprise she was not screaming. Her eyes widened and she stared up at him. After a moment, her mouth opened, but no sound came out.

Madison stared wide-eyed. She did not know what she had expected His Majesty to look like, but not what he did, that she was certain of. It had never even entered her head that he would look like that. She was trying desperately to remember the word for what that was, but right this minute and in her stunned state, her brain had flatlined. A moment later her mouth fell open and she continued to stare. Finally she remembered – a werewolf. She closed her mouth. His Majesty was a werewolf. *During the day? Were they still called a werewolf if they were out during the day?* She did not know. She had never been into horror movies. Her life was horrifying enough, she did not need movies to scare her. He towered over her standing on his hind legs. He definitely looked like some bizarre combination between a human and a wolf. His snout was not as pronounced as that of an actual wolf. This was made more ridiculous than scary by the expensive looking britches and tunic he wore. The tunic was crisp white with embroidery around the collar. His sleeves were rolled up to just below his elbows. He also had on a gold necklace with a medallion, and on each wrist were gold cuffs. His coat was silky black and he had steely gray eyes, but perhaps the most surprising thing about him was the fact that he was solid just like her. It felt strange seeing someone live and in color after having dealt with ghosts for the past couple of weeks. As she continued to stare at him, she had to admit his steely gray eyes watching her intently was making her uncomfortable. He gave the impression of being ready to pounce and she was quite certain had she made so much as a peep, she would be halfway to the river right now.

Mathias continued to stare at the woman. As of yet, not a single sound had escaped her lips, but at least she closed her mouth. He sniffed. Clearly she had been using some of Margaret's lemon soap. He sniffed again. She did not smell nearly so revolting; in fact, she almost smelled human. He sniffed several more times, but she still did not smell like a woman. He appraised her appearance. She was in a very nice, deep purple gown and a silver bodice. She wore no jewelry. Now properly clothed, he had to admit she at least looked like a woman with her blonde hair neatly braided and her blue eyes staring up at him.

Madison finally recovered and said, "It occurs to me I should bow or curtsy or something, but I don't know what is proper and I certainly don't know how to curtsy."

He snorted. "Do they not have Kings where you are from?"

"In other countries they do, but not in mine. We have a President."

"What is a President?"

"An elected official, the people vote him into office."

He blinked. "That sounds truly horrible. People are stupid and do not know what is best for them."

"So you think anyone who is not noble is stupid?"

He snorted again. "That is not what I said. I said people are stupid, a person is intelligent."

She considered that for a moment, then nodded. "Alright, I'll grant you that point."

Mathias could not help it, he laughed and gave her a mock bow. "How gracious of you, My Lady."

"I'm not a lady. I guess I would be considered peasant riffraff."

He considered that for a long moment. "Well, given the fact that you are a foreign visitor, it only seems proper to give you the courtesy title of Lady. After all, we cannot insult our guests."

"Am I a guest, or a prisoner?"

"You never answered my question. How did you come to be here?"

She shrugged her shoulders. "Theft and assault."

"Someone stole something from you and assaulted you? That does not make sense."

"I'm assuming it was you who spoke with my brother and told him he had to return. That you'd send him home to say goodbye, but he had to return." He stared at her wide-eyed, then nodded dumbly. "Well, my brother came to me to say goodbye and explained everything to me. I couldn't let him be taken away from his family, they need him, you see. Barbara's a stay-at-home mom and the boys are in high school, a junior and a freshman. Kelly is just starting middle school. They need him. I don't have anybody but Charles, so I rendered him helpless, took the stone, and came myself."

"You rendered your brother unconscious? What did you do, hit him from behind? No, forget that, you could not even reach."

She put her hands on her hips and looked annoyed. "I'm not that short, and besides, I used a stun gun."

"What is a stun gun?"

"Imagine a handheld device that when you push a button releases a lightning bolt, and if that is pressed up against a person, they get the lightning bolt."

He nodded with approval. "That would work. Is this not fatal?"

"It's considered nonlethal self-defense."

He frowned. "That seems ridiculous. Why would one want self-defense to be nonlethal?"

"That gets really complicated. Let's just say in my world there are the liberals and there are conservatives. The liberals believe everybody should be left alone to their own devices and the world shall be happy and friendly. The conservatives believe that nobody's going to get along, so you better stand up and defend yourself, or something to that effect."

"That sounds like insanity personified."

She considered for a long minute. "Given everything that's going on in my world, I would have to agree with that, but that does bring us back to the fact that I am here in my brother's place. So if you were going to hold him prisoner, I guess I'm your prisoner."

Mathias was still finding it impossible to believe that the small woman in front of him had overpowered the man he had met, taken the stone from him, and traveled here. He was looking at her in a whole new light. "Whether you are treated as a guest or a prisoner is entirely up to you. I will permit you the freedom of the Castle and grounds, but you are not to stray beyond the walls. Just because there are gaps does not mean that you can cross them. As far as you are concerned, the wall is complete and intact ..." He indicated it with his hand as he spoke "... and any time you come upon a fallen section like this, stay away from it. It is dangerous."

She nodded. "That seems quite fair, Your Majesty."

"It occurs to me we have not been introduced. How are you called?"

"Madison Rose Brewster."

He inclined his head. "I am King Mathias of Glacier Guard."

Again Madison felt like she should curtsy or something, but she did not know how, so instead she gripped her skirt and bent her knees.

He rolled his eyes and snorted, turned on his heel and walked away, tossing over his shoulder, "Tomorrow morning after breakfast, you will begin etiquette classes with Louisa."

XI

The following morning, Madison awoke when someone yanked open the curtains. It was not only the noise, but the sudden bright light that startled her into consciousness. She sat up and looked around. Gretchen placed her breakfast tray on her lap. "Good morning, Madam. Did you sleep well?"

"I did, thank you." Madison watched Gretchen move about the room, adjusting things here and there. She still found the inhabitants of the Castle quite unusual. On an impulse she asked, "Why are all the inhabitants of the Castle translucent? The Castle itself is solid and His Majesty is solid, not to mention why is he a werewolf? Are there other people in this realm who are wolfmen? And if so, why are there no other ones here in his kingdom and y'all are like normal people?"

Louisa said from the doorway, "Lesson one of good etiquette: a lady does not ever say 'y'all are like normal people'. Is that even proper grammar where you are from?"

Madison blushed and looked down. "My mother would say no, my generation would say yes."

Louisa made some kind of noise that clearly indicated, 'oh, I see', then said aloud, "Lesson number two: it is rude to question the servants about their master. It does not matter whether the master is a farmer, a lord, or King. If you have questions, you should ask him, not his servants."

"Yes, ma'am."

"Lesson number three: a lady does not ever sit there hunched over with her shoulders rolled forward and her head drooping. You look like a child, not a lady."

"Does it really matter how I am sitting? I'm in bed."

Louisa replied as she approached, "A lady is always a lady, whether alone, or surrounded by her peers." Arriving at Madison's side, she tilted her chin up, then began rearranging her body position until she was sitting properly. "Much better, concentrate on maintaining that posture. As soon as you have finished your breakfast, we will get you up, dressed, and we will continue this lesson in more detail. His Majesty would like me to report on how you are progressing tomorrow."

While Madison got dressed, she took this opportunity to study Louisa. She really could not believe she had not done this earlier, but her mind had been so muddled, she had not seemed to be able to hold onto a single thought. And when she was out of her head, the only time she had found peace was when Louisa was around, and then all she had wanted to do was sleep. But in the last two days, she had felt so much better, she had really found a new interest in life. She smiled. Louisa was short, though still taller than Madison, tending towards plump, with a warm and loving demeanor about her, and her hair appeared to be darker as did her eyes. Her age was very hard to determine. Madison thought she was about thirty but was not sure. She, too, appeared to be wearing some kind of dark blue or brown dress, but unlike Gretchen, she wore a white apron. "You know it occurs to me, I haven't thanked you for everything you've done for me while I've been here, and in truth I don't even know how long I've been here. It seems like only a few days to me, but it could have been more. I am sorry to be so much trouble."

She nodded and looked sad. "You have been here for a little over three weeks."

Madison stared in surprise. She could not believe that. It did not feel like that long. "I am so sorry I was so much trouble."

Louisa smiled and shook her head. "Do not apologize repeatedly, it is a nuisance. Apologize once and mean it." She waited until Madison was fully dressed, then she indicated the spot in front of her. "Stand there." Madison did as she was told. Louisa began walking slowly around her, speaking as she did so. "Chin up, but not out. Shoulders back without sticking out your chest. You are dropping your chin again. Head erect, back straight, feet together, your hands should be clasped in front of you. No, no, not that high. In front of your middle, yes, much better. Now today we are going to focus on the curtsy, walking, sitting, and tone of voice."

Madison was starting to think that being in the dungeon would be easier. Four hours later, she was convinced of it. Her shoulders were sore, her back ached, her head was throbbing, and her mind was reeling. She was convinced she was never going to learn this. It seemed as though everything she said was wrong, everything she had ever been taught was wrong, and she was sure wherever her mother was, she was laughing at her. She could not take it any longer, she rubbed her hip.

Seeing the gesture, Louisa asked with some concern, "Is your leg bothering you?"

"Yes, but I'm sure it will be all right."

"Why do you not follow me to the infirmary. It will give you a chance to get some exercise and I can give you a salve which I think will help with the pain."

Madison frowned. She was not sure about that. "I very much appreciate the offer but ... I don't ... do not want to the end up back on more medicine. I finally feel clear of it."

Louisa smiled at her. "This is not that kind of medicine, child. This is something you can just use when it hurts. I promise it will be all right."

She still was not sure about this, but she nodded. "Thank you." Louisa turned and the two of them headed for her infirmary. After a minute or two Madison asked, "So I understand that it is considered bad manners for me to question you about your master, but can I ask why he is making me do all this? I'm just a prisoner. Why do I have to learn how to be a lady?"

Louisa considered that for a minute or two. "I can answer quite truthfully. I do not know, but it is not for me to question, but to obey, and learning good manners will not do you any harm."

"Do you think he will keep me here forever, or send me home after a while?"

Louisa frowned as she considered that. In her personal opinion she thought that Mathias was going to be keeping her forever, but she decided it was better not to say this. Instead she replied, "Again, I do not know. There was a time when he confided in me, but that was a very long time ago."

Madison glanced at Louisa out of the corner of her eye, she looked very sad. She wondered if at one time they had been lovers. What a thought. She frowned and wondered how old the King was. It was impossible for her to judge, and Louisa was rather attractive. That was definitely something to occupy her mind and something told her she was going to need lots to think about.

XII

Madison stood clutching her sketchbook to her chest, looking across the countryside through one of the gaps in the wall. Today marked her sixth week in this realm and as of yet she had only spoken to His Majesty twice and still had no idea what he was planning to do with her. She sighed. Everything look so pretty on the other side of the wall, not that the Castle was not pretty, or the grounds. It was probably just her human nature longing to be where she was forbidden to go.

"You look very melancholy."

She started and turned. At sight of His Majesty, she sank into a curtsy. "Good afternoon, Your Majesty."

Mathias inclined his head. "Much better. Are you unhappy here?"

She started to shrug her shoulders and then remembered that a lady never replies with a shrug of her shoulders, a verbal answer is always required. "As a prisoner, I can have no complaints."

"Do you really consider yourself my prisoner?"

"That is difficult to answer. On one hand, I am most definitely your prisoner; after all, I am confined within these walls, but on the other, you are quite correct. It seems ludicrous to call myself a prisoner when I am well fed, clothed, warm, and comfortable, and the happiest I've been in years, if not in my entire life, and I feel better than I've ever felt. It is probably just the restless nature of man that makes me feel imprisoned since I cannot cross the walls."

He considered that, then nodded. He turned to stare through the hole in the wall, gesturing as he spoke, "I can understand your feelings on the matter. Though you will probably not believe me if I told you there is really nothing on the other side of the wall worth seeing, a few villages, the villagers. Though they would be different people to talk to, the conversations amongst villagers is pretty much the same, the weather, the crops, fishing, hunting. You get the idea. The face may change, but the conversation does not vary."

She followed his gaze as she said, "Spoken like a true aristocrat."

"What is that supposed to mean?"

She turned back to the Castle. "It means you look down your nose on them because they are farmers, and they live in a hut, and you live in a Castle."

Mathias could not help it, he started laughing. "I see you have a very wrong idea of me. I would rather talk with farmers about farming every day of the week than carry on a conversation with my fellow aristocrats, as you call us. Now those are boring conversations. I was merely saying that in our small, closed in country, conversations do not vary much, and you tend to hear the same stories over and over and over."

She looked at him with some surprise. "I confess, I did think you preferred your own class to the lower classes."

He shook his head. "Not in the least."

They stood there in amiable silence for a few minutes. Finally she decided she was going to ask. Now was the time. "Why are all your people translucent and look like ghosts, and yet they can pick up and interact with things just as I can, and I can touch them. I do not understand."

"That is nothing for you to concern yourself with."

"Very well, Your Majesty. What do you intend to do with me?"

"You are my guest until I say otherwise."

"Prisoner."

He growled. "Do you delight in angering me?"

"I learned at a very young age not to be fooled by the lies people tell you, but to look through them to see the truth. I am not your guest. You do not want me here. I am your prisoner. You keep me here because ... why?" She turned to face him. He was glaring at her. She ignored his hostile demeanor. "Because you think I can solve some problem for you, that is why I am here. You said my brother was brought here for a purpose. You are trying to decide whether his purpose was me, or whether now that you have me, you have to figure out a way to get him instead."

He snorted and growled. "You are very cynical for one so young."

"Life has made me cynical."

He snorted and laughed. "Oh, yes, I am sure your life was so hard."

She glared back at him. "You know nothing of my life! Do not judge others until you have walked a mile in their shoes!"

He replied with great amusement, "I could not possibly walk anywhere in your shoes. They are way too tiny." He held his thumb and his index finger about an inch apart. "Just like your perceived hardships in life, very tiny. I mean really, what made your life so unbearable? I mean was the husband Daddy chose for you too old, or was it the fact that he merely expected you to sit there and remain silent."

Madison gripped her hands tightly in front of her, telling herself over and over again, *A lady never raises her voice and lady always remains calm.* She tried to convince herself that what she was telling herself was true. It was not working.

Mathias started laughing. "See, you cannot even think of anything, can you?"

That was it. Madison saw red. She screamed at him, "You can't even begin to imagine what it is like to have your hip replaced and then to outgrow it, and have it replaced again and again, then to have to learn to walk again and again, and to have someone decide that they can make your leg longer, and to put bolts and rods and screws into your leg, and then how it feels when they turn them to try to make your legs longer. Then every time you go back to school to have everybody point and laugh because you are the middle schooler with a walker, and then you are the middle schooler on crutches, and with a cane, and somehow through it all you manage to keep one friend …" Tears were now streaming down her cheeks, but she did not care. "… But then high school comes and he gets taller, and then suddenly discovers that he can be cool, and so he starts changing how he dresses, how he looks. Which is fine with you. You are happy for him, right up until he is in with the cool crowd, and in order to stay in with the cool crowd he has to make that one little joke about you. Then the one friend that you've had through all the surgeries, and all the pain, and all the torture, looks right at you, and laughs, and says to his new friends that if they ever needed an easy score, that I was such a low hanging fruit they could get me with a little dog food. You're right. In the grand scheme of things my problems are so small, but that doesn't mean they didn't hurt." She dropped her sketchbook and fiddled with her handkerchief as she started wiping her eyes.

Mathias was staring dumbstruck. Despite his not understanding half of what she had just said, he understood enough to know that her life had not been easy, and he had even known that before he had goaded her, but he had been so desperate to draw her attention away from him. He knew he should apologize, it was the gentlemanly thing to do, but he had never been one for apologies. He continued to stare at her. She angrily wiped her tears away, trying to stop crying. Then he caught a glimpse of something. He reached out like lightning, grabbed her left wrist and pushed her sleeve back. As he turned her hand over palm up, he demanded, "What is that?" He tentatively ran a claw along the long scar starting at her wrist going towards her elbow. It was about three inches long.

Madison squirmed and twisted, trying to wrench her hand free. "None of your business."

Mathias did not know why, but on an impulse, he let go of her left wrist and grabbed her right. He pushed her sleeve back. There was an identical scar. She continued to struggle against him. He growled, "Stop it." She stopped and glared at him. He gripped her other wrist and turned it over, staring at both scars, he said slowly, "You did this to yourself. You tried to kill yourself. Why would you do that?"

Madison's shoulders slumped and she sighed. "Believe me, looking back on it now, it sounds pretty pathetic, even to myself, but I was hurting all the time. Mother and Father were discussing trying another specialist to extend my leg. Marco had just become cool and the entire school was talking about what an easy lay I was. It just seemed like a good idea. I had it planned perfectly. It would have worked, but fate intervened, which I'm really glad it did. Mother and Father were going out of the country for the week, and I was going to be alone, and it was the housekeeper's night off. Charles did not live at home anymore. He was married with children of his own. He's seventeen years older than me, in case you did not guess. I really do not even remember him living at home. He went to college when I was one, but he decided he wanted to come over and see me. So he picked up a pizza and rented a movie so he could hang out with his baby sister. I do not think he's ever has forgiven me for finding me on the kitchen floor in a pool of my own blood. Can't say as I blame him for that. But that's okay, I kind of harbor a grudge for him putting me in the madhouse, because Mother and Father were already on a plane, and they were going to Paris. So needless to say they could not be bothered to come back and deal with their crazy daughter, so Charles had to do it all. When they released me from the hospital, he took me to the madhouse. I mean it was a nice one, but pills and group therapy were their solution to everything. That was Mother and Father's solution to everything as well. Pills made everything better. I think

Mother and Father had determined they were just going to leave me there, but Charles got me out, took me home with him for a while until I got my own place, and then he called me every day, and has pretty much talked to me every day since then, until I came here."

She had ceased struggling, so he released her. He asked gently, "What are pills?"

She sighed. "In my world there are three ways to administer medicine, a syringe, which is like a tube with a needle and they push it into your body, pills, or liquid."

"What did these pills do? What was their purpose?"

She crossed over to one of the fallen stones and sat down. "Well, let's see. They gave me pills to make me happy, pills to keep me calm, pills to counteract side effects from other pills, pills for the pain, pills to make me sleep, and of course, birth control."

He sighed and sat down next to her. "What is birth control? It sounds positively horrible."

She laughed and shook her head. "You are something else. What do you think it sounds like?"

"It sounds as though something a woman would take to ease her labor pains to control the birth."

"Not even close. It is actually to prevent her from getting pregnant in the first place."

Mathias stared in horror. After a moment he demanded, "Is such a thing even legal?"

"Has been since the 1950s, or so I'm to understand."

"Women do this on purpose? Why?"

"As I understand it, it is all part of the feminist movement. Women wanted to have a career and be able to behave and act like men, which meant sex without consequences."

"What benefit is there in being like a man?"

"I guess women of my world believed that they were second-class citizens and they wanted the same rights as a man."

Mathias started laughing. "That just sounds dumb. Why would a woman want to be a man's equal? A husband is supposed to take care of his wife, fathers their daughters, brothers, their sisters. It is our responsibility to feed you, clothe you, take care of you, and see to your well-being. Why would you want such responsibility? It is a man's job to work, to put food on the table. It is a woman's responsibility to stay home and to raise the children. It is a balance. So you do not want a family? Very odd. And what is this career?"

"A career is a trained skill like a blacksmith, only appropriate to my world. And no, I never wanted one ... a career that is, but yes, I have always wanted a family. But that is all more of the drama which is my life that you really do not care about. So, did your mother raise you? Are even Queens supposed to raise their children?"

"My mother, no, but she hates me, so not exactly surprising."

"Your mother hates you? Surely she did not always hate you?"

Mathias started laughing. "My mother hated me before I was even born. According to my father she prayed every day for a miscarriage. I am stubborn, I was born anyways. My brother, she loves him. She treated him well or as well she treated anybody."

She looked at him in surprise. "Why did she hate you? She sounds like a truly awful person."

Mathias rubbed his hands up and down his face. He was not sure he wanted to get into this, but since he had questions he wanted to ask, it seemed only right to answer hers. "My mother was engaged to be married to another prince, but my father saw her and wanted her for himself. Wait a moment, I am getting ahead of myself. Their two kingdoms ... Our two kingdoms, Glacier Guard and Rivers Edge, were then and still are at war with each other. I think largely my father kidnapped her out of spite.

My father had agreed to go and sit in on peace negotiations between three kingdoms, Glacier Guard, Rivers Edge, and Oak Fortress. The talks were not going well. There were two other kingdoms that were there as mediators, Dagger Drop and Sky Haven. The Prince of Sky Haven was my mother's betrothed. Finally, the Prince of Oak Fortress had enough and stormed out. My father decided to follow his lead. The only difference is my father took something with him when he left, mainly my mother. My mother and father paint very different stories on how that all went. According to my father, my mother was not exactly thrilled about marrying the Prince of Sky Haven, so she did not object too much the first few nights. But by the time he made it back here, she hated him for ruining her and taking her away from her family. At this point my father had no intention of giving her back and their marriage was basically horrible from that moment on, and they were not even married yet. Apparently I came along pretty quickly. According to my mother, my father kidnapped, raped and beat her and held her prisoner. He did not give her a moment's peace until he was certain that she was carrying me, and then he locked her in her room until I was born and kept her prisoner until the day he died. I have no idea what their marriage was like. I was restricted to the nursery until I was ten. Though I saw my father most days, my mother did not start coming around until Jared was born and I was seven then. But as I understand it, noble marriages are usually awful."

"Gee, and I thought my mother was horrible. Mine apparently does not have anything on yours. I am sorry. What was your father like?"

"He was a good King, a good hunter, a good leader of his people, a good protector. According to my mother, a terrible husband. A good father, he cared. He saw Jared and I nearly every day of our lives. He taught us what he thought was right and wrong. He was very kind, very loving, and would take us out and do things with us, teach us things. He taught us what we needed to know, how to hunt, how to ride a horse. We were not left to the servants all the time."

"When did he die?"

"When I was sixteen, but he made sure I was ready to take the throne. When did your parents die?"

"About three and a half years ago, a little before my seventeenth birthday. Mother and Father were going to Colorado to do some skiing. Father was a pilot. The weather reports were bad, but father said he'd flown in worse and took off anyways. The airport had grounded all commercial planes, yet they just advised all private planes against taking off under those conditions. Fortunately Mother and Father had not taken anyone with them this time, so the only people who died were them. That's when …"

"That's when, what?"

She got to her feet and shook out her skirt. "That is when Charles became my legal guardian, because before Mother and Father died they had me declared mentally incompetent and no matter how old I get, I will always have to have a guardian." She dropped into a curtsy, turned, and hurried away.

Mathias slowly shook his head. "Whatever fates decide what realm you are born to, thank you. I am very glad I was born in this one."

XIV

One week later, Mathias sat in his office, drumming his fingers on his desk. He found the more he learned about Madison, the more questions he had. After some consideration, he thought he had translated some of her expressions well enough. He ran his hands up and down his face and demanded of himself, *Why, why did the witch bring Charles here? Why bring Madison here? Which one of the coven is responsible for all of this?* He opened his desk drawer and pulled out the pendant. He held it up and frowned as he considered it. *And why is the pendant still here? Why has she not reclaimed it? These women do nothing without a purpose. What is their purpose?* He drummed his free hand on the desk. *Okay, let us consider that for a minute. Why do they usually do anything? To maintain the balance, to administer justice, to punish, to aid, or to reward.* He mulled all of that over for several minutes, then he decided to attack each one individually.

He retrieved a fresh sheet of paper, opened his inkwell, dipped his pen, and then carefully wrote, 'Balance, Justice, Punishment, Aid, Reward', giving each word its own line. Then began tickling his chin with the quill. *I can think of no way in which Charles or Madison assist in maintaining the balance.* He drew a line through 'Balance'. *Justice, however, merits possibilities. Maybe Madison deserves justice, but why put her here?* He put a check next to 'Justice', then leaned back in his chair and continued to rub the quill along his chin. Again he could think of no reason why the coven would desire to punish Charles or Madison. *Charles had clearly always done the best he could for her, but being a brother, his options were limited. Which could mean the purpose is to punish me. Does it punish me? As of this moment, no.* He did nothing to 'Punishment' and moved on. *Clearly Madison needed aid. The realm she came from was crushing her soul, but again, why bring her here? Charles in no way needed aid.* He sighed and placed a check next to 'Aid'. Again, he could think of no reason why either one of them would be brought here as a reward. *It seems more like a punishment.* He dipped his quill in the ink again and drew a line through 'Reward'. At the top of the page he wrote, 'Charles and Madison', requiring them to share a line. At the very bottom he wrote Mathias. *The three of us have to be connected, this cannot be a coincidence.* He closed his inkwell and threw his quill on his desk, then he rubbed his hands up and down his face again. He said aloud with great irritation, "I need more information."

"If it is information you seek, perhaps I can help you."

He groaned. He hated when he forgot and spoke aloud in his office. He kept telling himself he should just move his office, but something told him that damn painting would appear on the wall of his new office. He had moved the painting multiple times, but it always reappeared hanging on his office wall. He had on numerous occasions tore it to bits, but it returned the next morning completely unharmed; however, he had learned if he did minor damage to it, it took a long time for that to repair itself. He did not know why, but it was amusing to occasionally cause minor damage to his mother. "There is no information I need from you. You are completely useless." He got to his feet and headed for the door.

"Now see here, Mathias, that is no way to speak to your mother, and if you will not respect me as your mother, at least respect me as the Queen Mother of your kingdom."

"I give you all the respect and deference that a painting deserves." Reaching the door, he opened it, crossed through it, then slammed it. He headed for the garden. As soon as he was outside, he sniffed the air several times. Catching her scent, he used his nose and found Madison in only a couple of minutes. Since arriving, her scent had changed so much, she now smelled like a normal human, and she was even starting to smell like a woman. He considered that for a minute, that might not be such a good thing. He approached her quietly from behind. He looked over her shoulder. She was sketching the Castle. He growled, reached over her shoulder, and yanked the sketchbook out of her hand. He did not hesitate as he ripped out the sketch she was working on.

Madison got quickly to her feet and turned around. She stared and then her jaw dropped. It took her a full minute to recover, and by the time she found her voice, he was in the process of ripping out another of her drawings. She screamed, "How dare you! That is mine!"

Mathias ignored her as he flipped through her sketches, removing several more. When he finally determined that there were no other offensive drawings, he handed her back the sketchbook. "You will not do any sketches of the falling down parts of my Castle, is that understood? And you certainly will never draw another sketch of me. Do I make myself clear?" As he spoke, he tore the sketches into shreds.

Madison wanted to scream at him. She clutched her sketchbook tightly to her. Finally she forced herself to sink into a curtsy and said coldly, "As you command, Your Majesty." Then she turned and started to walk away.

Mathias snapped, "You are not dismissed. I permitted you to leave last time without my permission, I will not do so today. Return this minute!"

Madison stopped, took several deep breaths, then turned on her heel and walked back. She said through clenched teeth, "Yes, Your Majesty."

"I have some questions about our conversation the other day."

"Clearly I do not have a choice, so please go on."

"I do not understand something. You and that boy Marco were lovers, so why did the two of you not have a family? You said you wanted a family. You clearly did not want to be using this birth control, so why were you?"

She dropped her sketchbook on the rock she had just been sitting on, crossed her arms over her chest, and asked coldly, "And explain to me exactly why any of this is your business? And besides, I thought ladies did not discuss such things, and I thought gentlemen did not discuss the intimate affairs of a lady."

Mathias snapped, "You were warned to answer my questions and to not ask your own in return!"

Madison smiled. "I am not one of your subjects. You cannot merely order me about."

He snarled, "I can throw you in the dungeon and put you on bread and water." To his annoyance, she pressed her lips tightly together and held her wrists out in front of her, clearly daring him to do it. He growled and snarled several times. She did not look impressed. Finally he snapped with irritation, "Why are you not afraid of me?"

She laughed. "You will forgive me, Your Majesty, but I find the concept of a sterile operating room and doctors with masks over their faces and scalpels in their hands far more intimidating than you."

He sighed with irritation, then growled. "Very well, I am trying to determine why you are here."

Madison considered that for a long minute, then asked, "And you think my relationship with Marco might have something to do with it? That was years ago."

"How many years ago?"

She sighed. "Four years ago and we were not lovers. I said we were friends, and I actually meant that, friends."

He frowned. "If you were not lovers, then why were you even on this ...?"

"Birth control? Why do you have such a difficulty with this concept?"

"Because it is beyond me why any woman would want to use it. After all, it is the nature of man not to buy what he is getting for free."

Madison started laughing. She was laughing so hard she had to grip her sides. It took her a minute to recover. "Oh my God, you sounded just like my father."

"Are you telling me that our two realms actually have something in common? That is a first, but I dare you to dispute my point."

Madison considered for a minute, then shrugged her shoulders. "In all reality, I cannot. Besides, the divorce rate in my country is like fifty-two percent, though actually the divorce rate is falling, but that is actually not because people are staying married. It is because they are just not getting married, which kind of actually proves your point. If a woman is already living with him, why is he going to marry her?"

Mathias crossed his arms over his chest and shook his head. "Are you telling me fathers are permitting their daughters to live with a man outside of marriage? I would kill her – after I killed him, of course. But moving on, though this is tremendous insight into the realm in which you come from, we are straying from the point."

"Fifty years ago, fathers would have and did agree with you. Nowadays, either they do not care anymore, or they have just chosen to remain silent. But you did not answer my question, why do you think my relationship with Marco has anything to do with this?"

"I am merely trying to gather facts so that I can understand you, because maybe if I understand you, I can understand why you are here."

"All right, I hate it, but that actually makes sense."

He gave her a mock bow. "Lady Brewster is so gracious."

"Can you at least call me Madison?"

He inclined his head. "If that is what you wish, but I must confess it would be very strange for me to be calling you Madison and you to continue to call me Your Majesty. You may call me Mathias."

She sighed and picked up her sketchbook and sat down on the rock. "Well, as I said, Marco and I were just friends. He was just the only one I had. I was never interested in the things other girls were interested in, but if you really think this will help you understand me, my parents put me on it after I slit my wrists. Though that actually was not their ultimate goal, they tried something much worse."

Mathias stood there watching her. One long awkward minute stretched into another. Finally he asked gently, "What is worse?"

"They originally tried to convince a doctor that I was too mentally unstable to have children and that he should perform a full hysterectomy."

"You do realize I have no idea what that means."

She sighed. "It is a surgical procedure that renders it impossible for you to ever have children. Fortunately, he had no intentions of doing that on a sixteen year old girl without a serious physical medical reason, which I did not have. I was perfectly healthy in that way and so he prescribed me birth control pills. My parents were not happy with that, so they took me to another doctor and tried again. This one, however, was less amused than the first one. He actually reported them to CPS ... Child Protective Services, it's a government organization. They were currently under investigation by them when they were killed in the plane crash, and because of everything, my brother was made my legal guardian, and that pretty much gets you up to speed on all of my life drama. Now explain to me exactly how you think any of that is going to help you?"

Mathias shrugged his shoulders. "I do not know, but you do realize your parents were insane. They have to have been."

She laughed. "I think I was rather young when I discovered that they were crazy. I often wonder how Charles turned out so normal. Marco once speculated that our parents were not our parents. He was always of the opinion that Charles and I both were procured by our extremely wealthy parents on the black market baby scene. After all, Charles and I are nothing alike and we're also nothing like our parents, but who knows."

"Black market, something else I understand."

"I guess every realm has its underworld. So why am I not allowed to draw images of falling down parts of your Castle?"

"Because I said so. Can you think of any reason why the coven would have brought you or your brother here?"

"I do not even know what the coven is."

He sighed. "They are the nine witches that control this realm. It is said that they answer directly to God."

"Well, that is different. We just have God in our realm. Well, that is not exactly true. There are a lot of religions, and there are varying viewpoints on who this God person is, how many there are, and well, you get the idea. I only believe in one God, but I do not have an answer to your question. I am sure it was an accident, maybe somebody else was meant to be here?"

"The witches do not make mistakes and they do not permit accidents in their plans, but it is getting late, good evening." He turned to walk away.

"Why do you never dine with me?" He did not break stride but continued to walk away. Madison thought to herself, *Maybe I am here to break your bloody neck.*

XV

Madison was convinced she was slowly going out of her mind. There were times she was starting to think she had lost track of how long she had been here. She thought it was now ten weeks, but she was not entirely sure, they seemed to have no calendar, at least not one she understood. She had since learned though, for whatever reason, though they spoke the same language, their alphabets were nothing alike. She was making small strides forward in learning how to read, but it was coming along slowly. All of this compounded to make every day seem like the one before it. The only variations were what she was learning in etiquette classes, or the days His Majesty chose to intrude upon her solitude in the garden. She hated to admit it, but those were her favorite days. He may be a bit of an arrogant ass, but he did have a reason to be an arrogant ass. After all, he was the King, even if his kingdom was small. He also seemed to be a strange mix of kind and compassionate, ruthless, and uncaring. Maybe that came with the territory of being King.

Louisa sighed and shook her head. "You are not paying attention to the steps again, Lady Brewster."

"Sorry, I was thinking about the King. I know you said it is bad manners to question the servants about their master, but is it bad manners if I ask how he reacted to my arrival here? After all, I do not even know how I got here exactly. I keep forgetting to ask. It seems like every time I go to ask, something more interesting arises and I ask about that instead."

Louisa sighed and shook her head. "You do realize you are not unlike a child, determined to do anything to forestall the inevitable."

Madison continued trying to learn the steps as she said, "Well, I must confess it does seem rather foolish for me to learn how to ballroom dance, when there does not seem to be anyone to dance with."

"Because dancing is a required skill of a young lady, and His Majesty told me I was to educate you until he said otherwise. Your education is coming along rather nicely, and we have reached the period in which you should learn to dance. But in regards to His Majesty's reaction to your arrival, I do not see that there is anything inappropriate in my saying he was irritated in the extreme. After all, he was expecting your brother, but by the time I arrived, he was more concerned than irritated."

Madison raised an eyebrow. "Why concerned?"

"Well, you had a very nasty head wound and it was bleeding profusely. He had stripped you out of your wet things and he had discovered the scars on your leg. They displeased him greatly."

She turned around quickly, bringing her arms up to cover her breasts even though she was fully clothed. She stared wide-eyed as she demanded, "His Majesty undressed me?"

"Well, you would not expect him to leave you in cold, wet garments to catch your death now, would you?"

"Why were my things wet?"

Louisa shrugged her shoulders. "We still do not understand how the pendant that brought you and your brother here works. His Majesty deduced that it requires a fall to trigger it, which apparently does work. Whether that is the only means of activating it, we do not know. Since it is clearly the property of one of the coven, I do not wish to analyze it, and His Majesty does not have skill in that department. But from the wounds your brother sustained, I gather he fell through the trees. You, however, landed in the river and were either unconscious when you hit or are unable to swim. His Majesty dove in and pulled you do out."

Madison struggled to remember. "I have a vague memory of hitting what felt like a snow bank for a brief moment, and then rolling and landing in water. I thought I dreamed it, but I was never taught to swim. My parents did not think a gimpy leg and swimming went together. I guess I am lucky His Majesty was nearby."

Louisa laughed. "Luck had nothing to do with it. His Majesty and the land are connected. He always knows when someone is trespassing on his land, but you have delayed your dance lessons long enough. Come, perhaps a partner will better assist you to learn the steps." She moved to stand in front of Madison. "I will lead." The two began dancing.

After the third time Madison had stepped on Louisa's foot, she pulled free and said with exasperation, "It is hopeless. I will never learn to dance. I am just not coordinated. Now if you ever have a guest you wish to assault, I would be the ideal partner."

Mathias forgot that he did not want to draw attention to himself and roared with laughter. Both women turned to face him and he remembered. He inclined his head and decided there was nothing for it, he moved forward. "I think you just need a stronger partner. Someone better able to take you in hand."

They both curtsied. Madison said with irritation, "You make me sound like an unruly child." Louisa retreated.

Mathias chuckled, stepped up and took her into his arms. "Not unruly, merely headstrong, and Louisa is not a forceful enough personality to lead you."

Madison tried to resist, saying firmly, "Do not be ridiculous. You are twice my height, there is no way we could dance together."

Mathias maintained his grip on her hand and adjusted his grip around her waist as he led her into the dance. "As I said, forceful and resistant." She glared up at him. He smiled back as he continued to lead her through the dance. After a few more steps he said with a grin, "See there, you are dancing just fine."

Madison was annoyed to discover he was not wrong. They were gliding expertly around the dance floor. She said the first hostile thing that came to her mind. "So instead of an unruly child, I am a horse you have to break?"

He clicked his tongue at her. "No, no, do not be ridiculous. A man would be a fool to try to break you. You are the kind of wild spirit that should remain unbroken, much better to give you your head until you work out the fidgets, then you will settle down and be a much more amiable companion."

She was not sure how to take that, it almost sounded like a complement. After another minute she said a little meekly, "It appears I should thank you. You saved my life, so thank you."

"You owe me nothing, but if you do not know how to swim, I suggest you not go near the river. Though it is calm in some places, it can be quite treacherous in others."

Madison did not know why, but she was suddenly finding herself a little warm and her heart was pounding. She said quickly, "I never learned to swim. You need not fear me going near the water."

He replied without thinking, "Most of my kingdom is bordered by water, perhaps I should teach you to swim." Without meaning to, his mind immediately conjured up images of her very lovely naked body. He shook his head and jerked. He asked of himself, *Where did that come from?* He forced himself to focus on her face. That did not help. His eyes immediately drifted down and he was imagining her lovely pale skin with water running off of it. He shook his head again and demanded of himself, *What is wrong with you? You had thought she was unattractive the first time you saw her. Why are you now? What has changed?* He had no answer for himself, but all he knew was right now he could not get the idea of her naked body out of his mind.

He jerked free turned and stormed off. He did not permit himself to look back. He went straight for the safety of his office. He entered and slammed the door and leaned against it. After a minute he slammed his head backwards into the door several times. "Stupid, stupid, stupid! What was that all about?" He growled and rubbed his hands up and down his face. "I have no idea."

Rosemary started to open her mouth, but the little voice deep inside said, *Shut up you. Every time you offer him advice, he rebuffs you. Maybe if you remain silent, you will learn something.* She decided to listen to her own advice and bit her tongue.

Mathias groaned and realized he was shaking. He could not for the life of him figure out what was wrong with him, but he could not get the smell of her out of his nose, or the thought of her naked body out of his mind. It was driving him insane and it had just come over him all of a sudden. He demanded aloud, "Why? Why now?" He had no answer to that, then a thought struck him. *Oh no, maybe that is what this is all about, punishment. Punishing me, driving me insane with my thoughts, my desires. Making me want something that I cannot have.* He groaned and started pacing up and down the room. He told himself over and over again, *You have to stop this, Mathias. You cannot have her, no matter how tantalizing your thoughts and desires are.* He walked up to a blank section of wall and started banging his head into it, saying with irritation, "But all I can think about is putting her on her back, burying myself inside of her, and grinding my body into hers until I find my release."

Rosemary finally could not remain silent any longer. "Of whom are we speaking, that nasty little outsider?"

Mathias slammed his head into the wall one more time. He had forgotten not to speak out loud. He hated that. One of these days he might actually learn to keep his thoughts to himself. "This is not a good time to mess with me, Mother, and she is not a nasty little outsider. She is from another realm."

Rosemary snorted. "She is just a pathetic whore from another realm. Why not have her, take her, use her for your pleasure, and discard her. She is nothing."

Mathias crossed to the sheet and yanked it off. He stared at his mother incredulously. He demanded, "Seriously?"

"Yes, seriously. She is just a pathetic peasant. She is of no import in this realm or her own. I see no reason for you to even hesitate. Go to her room tonight and use her as you will. You are the King. She should be grateful for your favors."

He continued to stare at his mother. Finally, he crossed his arms over his chest and asked, "And you really think she is going to consent to go to bed with me as I am?"

Rosemary sighed and rolled her eyes. "As I keep saying, she is just a peasant whore. I doubt seriously you would be the first man to use her and discard her, nor the last, and if you are, so what? She is after all just a peasant, her consent is not needed."

He stared speechless for a long minute, then he snapped angrily, "You have told me my entire life that you hate me and my father because he kidnapped you, and according to you, raped you and imprisoned you, forcing his unwanted seed on you; and yet you would have me do the same to another woman?"

She snorted and rolled her eyes. "That is entirely different. The two do not even begin to compare. I was the Princess of Rivers Edge, not some dirty little peasant. I mean, really, Mathias, they sleep with the pigs and run around barefoot and half naked. Royal blood runs through your veins. She should be grateful for your attention, and it is not as though you would cast her off without compensation. You have already been looking after her, and if you desire to keep her for your mistress, so be it."

He could not believe what he was hearing. He had always known his mother was a bitch, he just did not realize she was heartless. He thought it was only him she had no love for, apparently he was very mistaken. After a moment he demanded, "Were you born without a single compassionate bone in your body, Mother?"

"I have compassion for those who are worthy of it."

Mathias turned and exited the room.

Rosemary sighed with irritation. She was going to have to come up with a way to deal with this. Clearly the boy was weak and was going to need some help. She wondered what she could manage in her current condition. She would have to think about that.

XVI

Madison was relieved that she had finally convinced Gretchen that she did not need her to put her to bed every night. She just could not get over the feeling that it was weird to have someone undress her, put her in the bath, dry her off, then put her to bed. It made her feel like a toddler. This allowed her to undress at her leisure, get in the tub, bathe, and just enjoy soaking in the hot water. Finally she dragged herself out and began drying. She went to the dressing table, picked up the brush, and began brushing her hair. When she was done, she neatly braided it, went back into the bathing chamber, and hung the towel to dry. She was just in the process of putting her nightgown on when she saw something appear on the dressing table. She crossed to it. It was a letter. It had her name on it written in the English alphabet. She frowned at that. She picked it up and opened it. It, too, was written in her own alphabet.

'Madison, I want to see you in my office immediately,

King Mathias'

She hesitated a moment wondering why he was summoning her in the dead of night, but something told her if she kept him waiting, he would turn into an anger ball, so she retrieved her robe, slipped it on, and hurried to his office. Though she had never been to it, she had a good idea of where it was. It was one of three doors that were off-limits, down the corridor that there was really no purpose in her ever going down, because all that was down it were those three doors, the formal sitting room, and the small study. Arriving, she hesitated. She thought she knew which one, but she found herself more than a little nervous. She opened the door and entered the room. It was lit by single lamp, but it appeared to be unoccupied. She closed the door and went to stand in the middle of the room. She wondered how long she was going to have to wait for him.

"You arrived much quicker than I thought you were going to."

Madison jumped and looked around. She had clearly heard a woman speak, but she had no idea where it had come from. After a minute she said, "I'm sorry I ... I don't see you."

"Enunciate, your grammar is atrocious, and do not be ridiculous, you looked past me twice." Madison looked around. Rosemary sighed with annoyance. "The painting, halfwit."

Madison turned and stared at the woman in the painting. She was a rather attractive, woman wearing an emerald green gown, with golden blonde hair. She was very slender and had sharp green eyes. Madison gave a little shiver as she stared at her. The woman instantly gave her the creeps. "I arrived faster than you thought?"

"Yes, I sent for you and signed my son's name. Well, I did not sign it; after all, I do not exactly have the ability to handle quills now, do I?" She held her hands out and wiggled her fingers.

Madison stared in bewilderment. Though she could move, she remained two-dimensional. It was actually rather disconcerting to look at. After a minute Madison asked, "Why did you send for me?"

"Because I wanted to see what all the fuss was about. I have to say, you are not much to look at, rather puny. Are you sure you are not a dwarf?"

Madison crossed her arms over her chest and asked, "And what if I am? It impacts you exactly how?"

Rosemary bored holes through her. "I am the Queen Mother, you will speak with respect when you speak to me, and anything that involves my son involves me."

"Well, I do not exactly involve your son. After all, I am merely his prisoner, and since I was specifically told to stay out of his office, and since I am not here at his request, I should be leaving."

Rosemary pointed at her. "You will stay where you are until you are dismissed. I thought you were attending etiquette classes. Clearly Louisa has completely lost her mind; otherwise, she would have informed you when dealing with royalty you remain where you are until you are dismissed. You will not talk back to me again. Believe me, I may be somewhat limited ..." She wiggled her fingers again. "... but I can make you feel my presence. Now, I invited you here for a proposition. Do you want to return to your own realm, or do you desire to stay here?"

Madison replied without hesitation, "I have no desire to return."

"Good, I can help you with that ..."

Madison interrupted, "And exactly how can you help me with that? After all, I am His Majesty's prisoner. I do not think he is going to be letting me return anytime soon and I am quite content to be his prisoner. I like it here. I have been in worse prisons."

Rosemary snorted. "Why am I not surprised? Well, if you want to stay here, you are going to have to help my son, otherwise, who knows what will happen to you. You may or may not have noticed that all of the Castle's inhabitants are somewhat ethereal. If the King does not get some help soon, I think it is very likely that they will be stuck like that for all eternity."

Madison did not know why, but something told her not believe a word this woman said, but she asked anyways, "And how can I help him? I do not have any magic."

"The King has always been the kind of man who holds his emotions in. He needs to let go and work off some of his pent-up frustrations. Frustrations you have only added to. If you care about the Castle or its inhabitants, you will help him deal with that."

Madison blinked. After a long minute she said, "Let me see if I translated that correctly. You want me to … screw your son, so he can find his own emotional ground zero again."

"I would not have put it in such a vulgar manner, but yes, I would like you to seduce my son. I have no idea what ground zero is, but if it makes sense to you and helps you to understand what I require of you, then yes."

Madison started laughing. "You are out of your mind. He hates me and the only reason he is keeping me around is he thinks I was brought here for a purpose. I am pretty sure he will never believe that purpose was screwing him, so that is a big no. As previously stated, Your Majesty, I was told that this room was off-limits, so good night." Madison sunk into a curtsy, turned, and headed for the door.

Rosemary screamed angrily, "How dare you turn your back on me! Do not walk out that door! I command you to come back!" Madison ignored her and continued walking. Rosemary said with amusement, "You were warned."

Madison gripped the door handle, then she screamed in pain and yanked her hand back, cradling it in her other hand. Her palm and fingers were badly burned. She stared down at her hand and bit her tongue, refusing to allow herself to cry.

"I told you I could make you feel my presence. Now, let us discuss my proposition. If you do as I tell you to do, I will make sure that you are quite handsomely compensated for any unpleasantness."

Still cradling her hand and refusing to look at the woman, Madison said coldly, "You may or may not understand this, but go to hell. I am sure your realm has some equivalent. Whatever part of the afterlife where you go to be punished, you can go there. I will not assist you in playing any games, and something tells me someone put you in that painting for a reason."

Rosemary shouted angrily, "You rude, disrespectful, little harlot!"

Madison started laughing. "Actually, if I was a harlot, you would probably like me better. Now I refuse to continue this conversation, please let me leave."

"You will do as I command you to do."

Madison ignored her and started banging on the door, shouting, "Help! Please, somebody, I am trapped in here!"

Only a minute or two had gone by when she heard a yelp from outside, then she started and stepped back as Mathias walked through the door, glaring at his hand. He stormed over to the painting and shouted angrily, "How many times have I warned you not to cause trouble in my Castle, old woman?"

"Mathias, I am your mother! You will not speak to me in that manner! But most especially not in front of others!"

Mathias leapt onto the low table and from that to the table against the wall in front of his mother's painting. She opened her mouth, but before she had a chance to speak, he raked his claws across her face, then he jumped backwards landing on the stone floor. He smiled as he watched her arms flail about, but no sound came out. He turned back to Madison and demanded, "Why are you in my office?"

With her good hand, she produced the note from her pocket and offered it to him. "I am sorry, but I received this. I did not know."

He took it, snorted as he read it, then tossed it over his shoulder. It burst into flames and disintegrated in an instant. The flames never reached the floor. He wrapped his arm around her waist, turned her in the direction of the door, and then the two of them walked through the door. He waited until they were on the other side, then said, "That was very foolish of you. You should have known I would not have sent for you at this hour, and you certainly should not have been wandering around the Castle in your nightdress." He led her down the corridor as he continued speaking, "I thought we discussed you not leaving your room unless you are properly attired."

"I know, I am sorry, but I did not want to risk angering you by leaving you waiting for an hour while I dressed." She frowned, then stopped walking and turned to face him. "I know you are probably going to tell me it is none of my business, but after my conversation with her, I am more confused than ever. What is going on here, Your Majesty?"

Mathias sighed and indicated her hand. "How bad is it?"

"Not so very bad, yours?"

"Fine, my hide is thicker than yours." He placed his hand on the small of her back and escorted her to the sitting room. He indicated the sofa. "Sit. Would you like me to send for Louisa?"

"No, I just want to know what is going on."

He seated himself across from her. He growled. "I guess that is fair and the answer is very complicated, but you once asked why I am the way I am, and my people are translucent, I believe that is what you called them. The answer to that is myself and my entire kingdom have been cursed. My mother, the charming individual that she is, is the one who did the cursing. As you may or may not have noticed, most everyone in my kingdom knows magic to some degree. That is true of all the kingdoms, but all magic is overseen by the coven and their rules. In cursing me and my kingdom, my mother broke these rules. The curse did not apply to her, but since she violated the rules, the coven put her in the painting and that is where she has been ever since. I have destroyed it on numerous occasions. Unfortunately she comes back the very next day, though I have learned to my great pleasure that minor damage like I just did takes much longer to be repaired than destroying it outright. Only in the mind of a witch does this make sense, but magic is one of those things that does not always make sense, kind of like curses."

Madison stared wide-eyed as he fell silent. After a long minute she asked, "What does the Castle falling apart have to do with all of this? You seemed very touchy about me drawing the damaged parts of it. It is connected, is it not?"

"Very much so. You may not have noticed, but all the damage to the Castle is at the corners, the towers to be precise. Two towers have fallen, and one is on the verge of collapse. I do not know this, but Louisa and I both speculate that if the curse is not broken by the time the fourth tower falls, my kingdom will be lost."

"What makes you think that?"

"The vines, they were not here until the curse. They started with the walls and the grounds and then they took out the first tower, then they spread to the second tower. They did not touch any other section of the Castle proper. When the second tower fell, they began spreading to the third. Again, they do not touch any other part of the Castle but the walls and the towers."

"How long have you and your people been like this?"

"You have not been here long enough to notice the seasons no longer change. I have measured the length of the day many times. The day is always precisely the same from sun up to sun down. It never changes, not a second. I believe, but I do not know, that we are frozen in that day, which makes it a little hard to track the passage of time. I believe we have been like this for a hundred and twelve years, but none of us would give you the same number, so I would say that we have all lost track of time. I think that is actually part of the curse, and it is a curse we cannot escape from, because we cannot leave my kingdom. The passes through the glacier froze over completely, preventing us from journeying outside of the kingdom. The river magically flows into other kingdoms, but if you try to go with it, you hit a wall of ice. So as long as you are in my realm, you are restricted to this kingdom."

She slowly shook her head. "That is terrible. Why will your mother not free you from this curse?"

He laughed, but it was a bitter sound. "Free us? She will not set us free. She wants us to stay exactly as we are. She wants the Castle to fall down around my ears. She wants me to suffer and she is succeeding."

She got to her feet, crossed over, and sat down next to him. "Then how do we break the curse? There has to be a way. What about the coven? Have you asked them?"

Again he gave a bitter laugh. "They would not help me. If they were going to do so, they would have done so long ago. The curse is unbreakable."

She reached over and squeezed his hand. "Nothing is unbreakable. If there is anything I have learned from watching TV, nothing is unbreakable. Maybe you are just looking at it the wrong way around."

Mathias looked down at her small hand on top of his, then he shifted his gaze to her. Before he knew what he was about, his arms went around her, and he pulled her against him. She looked up at him wide-eyed. He started forward with every intention of kissing her, but he froze about six inches away. He could feel her shaking with fear in his arms. He released her, got to his feet, and shouted angrily, "Louisa!" A long minute passed, then he yelled even louder, "Louisa!"

Louisa hurried into the sitting room. Her eyes widened and she stared in surprise when she saw Mathias standing with his back to her and Madison on the sofa. She curtsied. "Yes, Your Majesty?"

"Take her to her room and return to me. Attend to her hand first."

Louisa crossed quickly to Madison and gripped her by the arm. "Come, child, you should not be out of bed, and certainly not as you are."

Louisa pulled Madison towards the door. Madison was nearly to the door when she managed to say, "But wait."

Louisa whispered, "He is in a mood, best not to argue with him."

Madison wanted to argue, but she did not know what had just happened. Maybe he regretted the confidence. He was a very private man, maybe he thought she would see him as weak now.

Arriving at Madison's bedchamber, Louisa attended to her hand. "You should not have been wandering about the Castle as you are. In future, do not leave your room unless you are properly gowned and shod. You are in your bare feet. Now get into bed before you catch your death." Madison grudgingly got into bed and permitted Louisa to tuck her in and blow out all the lamps. "Good night, My Lady, get some sleep." Madison wondered how she was supposed to sleep. Her new home was falling down around her ears, all because some wretched, evil woman, who gave her the creeps, had cursed the lot of them. She was going to have to find out more about this curse, otherwise, she would not know how they could break it. In the movies, there was always some catch. She would have to find out what it was.

XVII

Mathias went to his office to await Louisa. He paced up and down the room feeling like a caged animal, wracking his brain trying to decide what the best thing to do was. By the time Louisa entered, he knew what had to be done. He turned and snapped, "Tomorrow morning as soon as she has had her breakfast, you will send her back."

Louisa stared, then demanded, "What?"

"Do not pretend as though you did not hear me."

"But why?"

"Do not presume to question me, do as you are told."

Louisa looked down at the floor. "No."

He turned and snarled at her. "You would disobey me?"

Still looking at the floor she said, "On this, yes. It is the wrong decision, Mathias."

He crossed to her and growled, "You will do as you are told."

"No, I will not, not this time. She belongs here. She was miserable there. They tortured and mistreated her, and you will send her back to a life of misery and torture." She could tell at once that he did not want to. She reached for his arm but remembered at the last minute and pulled her hand back. "Please, why do you do this? It is so unlike you."

He opened his mouth several times trying to find words, finally he said, "It is better for everyone if she goes."

"But you do not want them to hurt her anymore, so why would you send her back to them?"

He growled and pulled back, running his fingers through his hair. "Because I am becoming afraid I will hurt her. She is driving me insane."

Light dawned and Louisa nodded. "She is wreaking havoc with your animal senses, is she not? I was afraid of that. It is probably only during certain times of the month. Perhaps you two should stay away from each other while you get used to her new smell, but Mathias, I think your problem runs much deeper. If you send her away, you will be in misery."

He laughed bitterly. "Not nearly as miserable as I will be every time she looks at me with disgust or fear. I do not know which is worse."

She put her hands on her hips and demanded, "And what is that supposed to mean? Madison is anything but afraid of you."

"Maybe before, but just now when I held her in my arms, she was shaking with fear."

Louisa rolled her eyes. She did not think fear had anything to do with it, but it was probably best if she did not say that. He would not believe her anyways. This was one of those things that was just going to have to run its course, but she was becoming more optimistic by the day that Madison could finally get through to Mathias and break the curse. No one else had been able to. He had remained on his stubborn high horse about the entire matter. "Well, one way or another, the two of you are going to have to find a way to continue to live together, as I will not send her back to that place. You would hate yourself forever if I did. Perhaps a good night's rest and the cold light of day will improve your outlook."

He sighed and chuckled. He reached out to caress her cheek. He closed his eyes and growled as his hand went through her. "You would think after all this time, I would remember I cannot touch you."

She shrugged her shoulders. "I forget too. Please, go get some rest. Things will be better in the morning. They always are in the light of day."

XVIII

Madison had tossed and turned all night trying to figure out what was going on. She was convinced that no one was giving her the whole story. She needed more information. Mathias had clearly told her all he was going to tell her right now. Louisa and Gretchen said they would not tell her anymore, and if she could not get Louisa and Gretchen to tell her anything, none of the other Castle servants were going to. Which really only left one person, but Mathias had effectively silenced that person and nothing she said could be believed. She clearly had ulterior motives. She rolled on her back and rubbed her face. What was she supposed to do? For that matter, what could she do? These people had had a hundred and fifteen years or so and had not solved the problem. She sat up in bed as a horrifying thought struck her. How many years had it been since the second tower had fallen? She threw the covers back, got out of bed, washed, and began dressing. She was just finishing when Gretchen brought in her breakfast. She demanded, "When did the second tower fall?"

Gretchen momentarily looked stricken. After minute she said, "I am not sure we should be discussing that, Madam."

Madison sighed. "His Majesty told me everything. When did the second tower fall? Please, it is important."

"Well, I am not sure. I mean …"

Madison sighed and added. "I know every day is the same, and it is difficult to keep track of time. He told me that too. So take a guess, twenty years ago, thirty years ago?"

"Well, I think it fell around eighty years after this all started."

"When did the first tower fall?"

Gretchen answered quickly, "Oh, that I am certain of. Forty years to the day after the curse."

Madison felt sick to her stomach. A tower fell every forty years, and everyone maintained that they had lost track of time, but they said that they had been cursed for about a hundred and fifteen or so years. Which could mean, it could easily be a hundred and twenty years. That would be when the next tower would fall. She demanded, "Which tower fell first?"

Gretchen replied looking a little confused, "The Southwest Tower, then the Southeast."

Madison ignored her breakfast as she hurried from her room, heading for the main staircase. She hurried down the stairs and exited the Castle. She was nearly to the main gate when she turned around and looked at the two remaining towers. She turned to one of the guards and demanded, "Which tower was the Southwest?"

He pointed. "The rear left tower, Milady."

Madison shifted her gaze to the front right tower. That would be the Northeast Tower. It was almost completely covered in bougainvillea. She shifted her gaze to the left, it appeared to be untouched by the bougainvillea. She moved to the right tower. She hesitated as she got closer. Then she moved to within reach of the tower, she could see the thorns digging into the stones. She stared up. After a minute, she moved around heading for the garden and the Southeast Tower, or what remained of it. She did not get too near the pile of rubble. She did not need to. The vines were completely gone. Clearly they moved in and destroyed what they intended to destroy, and then moved on to destroy something else. She had never thought of bougainvillea as a destructive plant, but she was definitely seeing it in a whole new light. She crossed to one of the large fallen stones and sat down on it, weighing her options. This was a magical world. Everyone seemed to have magic. Could she use magic? That was an interesting question. She would have to consider that. Did she need magic? No, not really. Mathias had said that the coven was in direct communication with God, so maybe she just needed to get their attention. She got to her feet and went about her day, considering all of her options.

By the time she was in bed, she knew what she was going to do. She blew out her lamp, sat, and waited. When she felt that the Castle was quiet, she got to her feet, lit a single taper, and tiptoed down to Mathias's office. She stood outside the door and told herself, *I am not afraid of her. She has no power over me.* She entered but did not close the door behind her. Crossing to the painting, she pulled the sheet down. It was a rather gruesome looking the figure standing there, arms crossed over her chest, tapping her foot, giving off the demeanor of a very annoyed person, but her face was nearly obliterated by four wicked claw marks. Madison hesitated, trying to figure out what she was to say. Finally she decided on, "Coven, I know I am not of your realm, but I believe you can hear me. I need to talk to her. I need to hear what she has to say. Please restore the painting. Let her speak to me. I need her help." One long minute stretched into another. She said again, "Please, I know you can hear me. Please restore the painting." She stared in wonder as the painting slowly began to heal itself. After about a minute or two, it was completely restored.

Rosemary said with irritation, "About time." She looked down on the little dwarf. "Oh, it is you again. What do you want?"

Madison spoke carefully, not wishing to lie. "I do not want to be a prisoner here any longer. I desire my freedom. Tell me what happened here and maybe we can help each other. Surely you do not desire to remain in this painting forever."

Rosemary laughed. "As long as Mathias continues to suffer, I will remain here for all eternity. So the little dwarf wants to go home? What makes you think I would help you with that?"

"Do you really have anything better to do with your time, so why not help me?"

Rosemary considered that. She did not trust the little dwarf for a minute. She clearly was up to something, but maybe she could use her to her advantage. After a minute she asked, "What do you want to know?"

"Why did you curse Mathias and the Castle? What happened?"

Rosemary felt tears spring into her eyes. "That wretched animal murdered my son, and I did not curse the Castle, at least that was not my intention. As often happens with words spoken in the heat of the moment, they took on an unintended consequence. I only intended to hurt Mathias, and to protect everyone else from him. I mean, you see what kind of animal he is. God merely made his outside match his inside. It was not right that he be so beautiful, when he is so evil on the inside, but you probably have not seen what he looked like before." She gestured to her right. "One door down on the right is the Portrait Gallery. They are all labeled."

Madison did not believe what she was saying about Mathias, but strangely enough, she did believe that she had not intended to hurt the Castle. On an impulse she asked, "Do you know that the Castle is falling down? Two towers have already fallen and the third will fall any day now."

Rosemary gasped and put her hand to her mouth. "No, that cannot be!" Her mind was racing, trying to understand then she sighed and nodded. "Of course, Mathias is linked to the Castle. If the Castle falls, he will die. That will leave no heir. But I would not worry about the inhabitants, they will probably be freed from the curse when Mathias dies, such a cheery thought. You know, that is probably why you are here. Since Mathias cannot come in contact with any of the other inhabitants, you are here because he can impregnate you. You know, you would find yourself in a very good position. You would be Queen for all intents and purposes for sixteen or even eighteen long years. If I were you, I would use Mathias for your own means, and as soon as you know you are carrying his child, then kill him with a dagger to the heart. If you have not the stomach for the blood, use poison. I can tell you where to find some very good ones. That should break the curse and leave us all free to go about our lives and you carrying the heir. Just something to think about. I, of course, would do anything I can to help you."

Madison was too stunned to even feel shocked. She could not understand how any mother could speak so casually about someone murdering her child. She needed time to think and to understand what the woman had told her. After a moment, she said a little uncertainly, "I think you have the wrong idea about Mathias' interest in me. Good night."

Rosemary laughed. "You are a woman. He is a man. He does not have to have any real interest in you, he just has to use you to satisfy his baser needs. As with all men, one must learn to use that to your advantage. Think about my proposal."

Madison said quite truthfully, "Oh, I assure you, I will probably be incapable of sleeping tonight. I will be too busy thinking about this conversation." She exited the room, closing the door behind her. She hesitated a moment, then turned and entered the Portrait Gallery. Holding up the candle so she could read the nameplates, she found it interesting how many of the women had been positive frights. Several of Mathias's ancestors were obese, unattractive slobs. As she walked along reading the nameplates and studying the paintings, she was relieved to find that the dates were getting higher. Granted, she had no idea what year it was, but at least she seemed to be heading in the right direction. She was nearing the end when she came upon a painting, King Rodrick. He was a rather good looking man, broadly built with dark blue eyes and shoulder length black hair, but he did not look particularly happy. The next painting was dated twelve years later and showed an older and much happier Rodrick holding what appeared to be a two year old Mathias. She smiled. He was a rather attractive child. The next painting was dated six years later and showed a younger version of the nasty woman in Mathias's office, apparently her name was Rosemary, holding what appeared to be a one year old boy named Jared. Rosemary and Jared were both fair-haired and brown eyed. She moved on to the next painting, which courtesy of the nameplates showed a sixteen year old Mathias and a nine year old Jared. They both looked bored, but they were both rather good looking young men. As she moved on to the next painting, she stared wide-eyed. It was titled Coronation of King Mathias, age eighteen. He looked very austere and unfriendly, but despite this he was indeed an incredibly good looking man with steely gray eyes. She studied it for a long time, then she moved on to the last painting, which was of Jared at age eighteen. She stepped back and held the candle up so she could study the two brothers at the same age. They in no way looked like brothers. She could definitely relate, she and Charles did not exactly look like siblings either. She frowned and demanded of Jared, "Why do I get the feeling you could settle this entire problem?" She considered that for a moment, then her eyes widened. "Of course, if you are dead, there has to be a headstone in the graveyard. It is within the Castle walls. I know where I am going in the morning." She headed for her room, considering everything she had learned today.

She was up before the sun, dressed, and tiptoeing out of the Castle. She took the long way through the garden and carefully gathered two bouquets of flowers. The sun had already made its full appearance when she arrived by the cemetery gate. She entered and closed it behind her, then assessed the layout. Determining where the newer graves appeared to be, she headed for them. As she walked along, she read the names. She found it incredibly saddening that so many of them seemed to have died before they were adults. She knew that was how it was back in the Middle Ages. That is why people always had such large families, chances were more than half of them were not going to survive to adulthood. Suddenly she froze and stared the headstones. She could read them. She could read the nameplates last night too. They appeared to be written in her own alphabet just like the note, but Mathias had read the note. She closed her eyes and shook her head. She wondered if she would ever get used to the magic of this realm, sometimes it was more than a little disconcerting. After a minute she dismissed it and went on about her business.

She quickly learned this cemetery was for the royal family only and it was easy enough to identify the different kinds of headstones. Children received flat headstones, adult non-heirs received small headstones about eighteen inches high, what she would call the standard tombstone. The headstones for the heirs were about twice as tall, but still standard. Headstones for every queen were different, some had small statues, some were square, some had obelisks, but none were over four feet tall. Kings, however, were an entirely different story. There appeared to be no rules, other than the fact that they were all over four and a half feet tall. Finally she came to King Rodrick's grave. His headstone was a three by three square stone with his name, date of birth and death. In the center was a stone sword that the top of the handle appeared to be about five feet off the ground. She neatly laid one of the bouquets of flowers in front of it. She stared at the dates. She frowned. It said nothing else. He must have died not long after Mathias's sixteenth birthday, not that she knew when it was, but Mathias had said he had been sixteen when his father had died. And she seemed to recall that coronations often took years to plan, which probably explained why his coronation was when he was eighteen, but she was guessing. She moved over to one of the other king's headstones. It was rather verbose about the king. She moved back to Rodrick's and asked, "Why does yours say nothing? That is weird. Granted, this entire thing seems to be weird." Next to Rodrick's grave was a fresh grave. It appeared to have only been dug yesterday. The dirt mound on top of it must be at least ten inches tall, and there was no headstone, merely a wooden board, but at the top it said 'Jared'. At the bottom someone had roughly scratched his date of birth and date of death. She knew it was merely a place marker. She seemed to recall somewhere she had been told it took six to eight months before a tombstone could be put on a grave. The ground had to settle. She sighed. He had died ten days after his eighteenth birthday. She placed the bouquet in front of the wooden marker. "Well, that is incredibly disappointing." She stepped back and looked from one grave to the other. "You know, if either one of you could see your way into helping me out, I would really appreciate it. I know you both could. I feel like I am chasing my tail. If there is anything you want to tell me, this is the moment." No surprise, nothing happened. Though for some reason she did not feel as though last night's excursion, or this morning's was a complete bust.

There was something here, she just had to figure it out.

XIX

Mathias entered his office and headed for his desk. "Good morning, I hope you slept well, perhaps aided by a warm, soft body."

He froze halfway to his desk. He took a deep breath and let it out slowly. He turned and stared at his mother. The sheet was lying on the floor. He demanded, "Who uncovered you, and better yet, who fixed you? I was hoping for at least six weeks of silence!"

Rosemary laughed. "The dwarf came to pay me a call last night. Apparently she is not without magic; after all, as you can see, my face has been restored again."

He crossed to the sheet and picked it up. "I assure you she will never do it again!"

Rosemary held out her hands to stop him. "Wait, before you cover me up, I think we should have a conversation. Do you want to know what she asked me?"

He sighed and shook his head. "Whatever conversation she felt the need to have with you, I really could not care less about."

"Even if I told you she asked who would inherit if you were dead?"

He was just moving to jump on the table to recover his mother. He froze. "Why would Madison ask such a thing?"

"I think she might have her eye on becoming Queen, which given your current options, is not a bad idea. The Castle is falling down around your ears, or so she informs me, and I am quite confident when it goes, you will be dead. Such a delightful thought, but I do not like the idea of there being no one to inherit the throne. Especially when I did not put up with your father for as many years as I did to have a stranger sitting on his throne rather than my own blood, which really only leaves a grandchild. So why do not you and the little dwarf come to some kind of agreement and the two of you produce a son."

Mathias snapped, "Do not call her a dwarf again!"

"Oh, I am sorry, did I touch a nerve? What would you rather I call her, peasant whore?"

He growled. "If you have such a low opinion of her, why are you encouraging me to spill my seed in her belly?"

"Given the fact that you cannot reach outside the confines of this kingdom and everyone within the kingdom is untouchable, her womb is the only readily available one and I would rather that than nothing. So stop fighting your natural desire and do us both a favor, put her on her back and get to work.

You will enjoy it, and the kingdom will get what it needs to stabilize the throne ... an heir."

Still holding the sheet in one hand, he crossed his arms over his chest and demanded, "Has it completely escaped your notice, Mother, what I look like? Something tells me our two species are not exactly compatible, and do you think I would risk my child being born like this?"

Rosemary laughed. "Oh, please, the coven is nothing but a bunch of goody two shoes. Do you really think that they would punish your child for your sins? Your child will be born perfectly human, though probably somewhat stunted ..." She held her hands shoulder wide, palms toward each other, then moved them forward until they were about six inches apart. "But any heir is better than no heir, unless of course you want one of the other kingdoms to take over your kingdom, or worse, one of their second-rate spares."

Mathias chuckled. "Mother, has it occurred to you that we are all repeating the same day, though we have our memories intact? What even makes you think it is possible for her to conceive a child, let alone bear one? After all, she does have some health issues."

"She is clearly outside of the curse. She would have no difficulty in conceiving a child, and as far as her health issues, it is not necessary for her to survive the birth as long as the child does. I am sure you could order Louisa to make sure that happens; after all, she listens to you."

He could not help it, he laughed again. "Which only reinforces my point. If she is outside the curse, then she is going to grow old and die, as would my child. After all, they would be stuck in this realm, or in order for them to survive, I would be forced to send them back to their own realm, which basically makes your entire plan pointless anyways."

She smiled at him knowingly. "Really? How much of the Castle is still standing? How long have we all been like this? How much longer do you really have, Mathias, ten years, twenty? I think your son will survive just fine that long, and then he could marry a nice girl and produce copious amounts of offspring. But then again, can the dwarf …" She gave a little gasp and put a finger to her lips. "My mistake, would you prefer I call her peasant whore?"

Mathias growled and said with irritation, "Mother!"

"Right, I meant Madison. Can she touch the Castle inhabitants? If so, maybe your son could have a rather good time with the housemaids. Your father always enjoyed the housemaids. I am sure you did, too."

Mathias snorted. "It is not as though he got any warmth from you."

She rolled her eyes. "It was not warmth he wanted from me, but sons of good blood with the right connections and I gave him those. Your father at least understood how to do his duty, perhaps you should try to do your duty some time."

He shook his head. "I do not believe a word you say, Mother. Madison would not come here to ask you about who inherits if I die. I do not know why she was here, and frankly, I really do not care, but I will not play your games, Mother. And I will not doom her or any innocent child to this life of living damnation we all find ourselves in, thanks to you. I think that is exactly what you want, more victims to your hatred, anger, and your malicious will." He jumped up on the table and started to stretch out the sheet.

Again she held her hands palm out in a vain attempt to stop him. "Mathias, if you do not believe me, ask her. Ask her why she was here. Ask Louisa. Louisa will tell you there is no reason that girl cannot give you healthy sons. I bet you if you ask Louisa, she will agree with me." He covered her with the sheet. "You do realize this does not silence me."

"No, but my claws across your face will." He jumped off the table and exited his office. He hesitated for a moment. He did not know why he was hesitating. He was torn between Louisa and Madison. Finally, he decided on Louisa and headed for the infirmary.

She was sitting at her desk, grinding herbs when he entered. She looked up and smiled, then frowned. "You appear to be in a charming mood."

He sighed with frustration. "Apparently Madison repaired my mother's damaged painting. Why would she do that? Why would she want to talk to my mother?"

Louisa raised an eyebrow. "Madison has no magic. She could not have done it on her own."

"That is another thing that you can explain to me. How does she have no magic and yet she repaired the painting?"

"Are you sure your mother is telling you the truth? You know she cannot be trusted."

He ran his hands up and down his face. "That is the worst part of this, she actually thinks you are going to support her crazy idea."

"Madison?"

"No, my mother."

Louisa got to her feet and walked around the desk. She perched on the edge. "That is impossible. You know I never agree with that woman." She crossed her arms over her chest, then cocked her head to the side. "Though out of curiosity, what is her crazy idea?"

He shifted from foot to foot. "She thinks I should marry Madison and produce a legitimate heir. She says Madison is the only viable choice. I told her that was crazy. I do not even think Madison could have a child, not after what they did to her, and even were that not the case, I mean, look at me." He gestured to his face and then his body. "I mean she has already fled my presence once, and besides any child would end up … like me … not that I think for a minute a human and whatever I have become … could … have a child."

Louisa was more than a little stunned. She could not for the life of her figure out why Rosemary would want Mathias with Madison. She considered that for a moment, then nodded. Actually, she could think of a reason. Rosemary was arrogant enough to believe she could intimidate Madison into doing her bidding. She saw her as tiny and weak. She would be in for a very rude awakening. Madison would hold her ground unlike anyone else.

Mathias interrupted her thoughts and demanded, "Are you just going to sit there and nod, or you going to agree with me?"

She held her hands out to either side. "Mathias, I can neither agree with you or disagree with you. On one hand, she is not wrong. Madison is a suitable choice and I see no reason Madison cannot have as many children as she wants. Labor might be more painful for her, but I think she will get through it just fine. And I doubt seriously your child would be born …" she indicated him, "… as you are. I think it would be a perfectly normal human baby. It is not the practice of the Coven to punish innocent bystanders. If you truly believed your mother's suggestion was ludicrous, you would not now be asking my opinion. You came here for me to agree with her, not to disagree. I think you have a very definite problem, but what you perceive the problem is and what I perceive the problem is are not the same."

He interrupted her and demanded, "And what exactly is that supposed to mean?"

"I think it all comes down to denial."

Mathias threw his hands up in the air, turned and stormed out, tossing over his shoulder, "I am truly in the fiery pits of damnation when you agree with my mother."

XX

Madison had no idea why, but she was now standing back on the east side of the Castle. Shifting her attention from the Southeast Tower to the Northeast Tower, she had thought it would give her some perspective. It was not working. All it was doing was making her feel panicky. She knew that there was no more information to be had, but since she could think of nothing else, it seemed as good a place as any to stand and be idle. After a moment longer of twiddling her thumbs, she focused on the falling down tower and headed towards it. Arriving, she frowned and reached out and ran her hand along one of the stones. "This all just seems so pointless. What is the purpose?" She stood there chewing on her lower lip. "Okay, curses are something from a fairy tale. Of course, they can always be broken, but one has to know how to break them, but then again, that is in a fairy tale and this is reality. Reality never has happy endings." She felt tears slide down her cheeks. Closing her eyes, she prayed to God for guidance. She reached out and rubbed one of the stones. She knew they had the answer. They, of course, heard everything. That was the advantage of being the walls. They, of course, knew everything. "If only you could talk." Another moment passed, then she felt an arm wrap around her waist, and she was jerked off the ground. She screeched and squirmed.

Mathias said angrily, "I think I have been a fair and reasonable man. I have given you very few restrictions and yet today you seem determined to break them all." He set her down on her feet. She turned and glared up at him. He demanded, "What do you have to say for yourself?"

"And exactly what rule was I breaking standing there?"

He put his hands on his hips and glared back at her. "I distinctly remember telling you that if you came upon a falling down section of the Castle to stay away from it. It was dangerous, and here you are handling the stones of the falling down tower. Are you trying to get yourself killed?"

"So what if I am? I am nothing but your prisoner."

Mathias threw his hands up in the air. "For the love of God, are we back to that? You are not my prisoner! The only restrictions I have put on you have been for your own safety, or my privacy. I am allowed a little privacy, am I not? Yet you were in my private office this morning."

"It was not this morning, it was last night. And all right, I will admit I did somewhat intrude upon your privacy, but I needed answers and you seemed reluctant to give me anymore, and Louisa and Gretchen would not give me any because you are the master ..." She held her hands out to the side and made quote marks as she said 'master'. "... So I saw no alternative but to question the one person who did not seem to care about hurting your precious feelings. I was trying to help. Since you are convinced I am here for a purpose, you should appreciate that."

Mathias growled several times, trying to think of something he could protest. "Using my mother as a source of information is not recommended given the fact that she is a born liar and out to get me. I would sooner have you question anybody but her."

She laughed. "Then perhaps you would be so good as to inform the rest of the Castle that, then maybe I might get somewhere. But as far as your mother being a born liar is concerned; generally speaking, if you know someone is a liar, they can still be quite helpful. You just have to remember they are a liar. Believe me, I never lost sight of that when talking with her. Kind of hard to believe anything that comes out of her mouth, but it was quite easy to determine what her objective is, given everything that she said."

He crossed his arms over his chest and demanded, "Oh, really? Enlighten me."

"To begin with, she does not want the curse broken. She would rather remain in that painting for all eternity than see you free, though I do believe that she actually did not mean to hurt the inhabitants of the Castle. I think that was an accident, but on the same note, I think she would burn the entire Castle to the ground if it hurt you. In the end, what she desired was for me to seduce you, get pregnant, and then kill you. Then I think her plan is for me to be her puppet on the throne until her grandson is old enough to become her puppet, but I could be wrong. However, she does actually believe that at your death the curse will be broken. I hate to say it, but I kind of agree with her on that; however, I do not think it has to come to …"

Mathias had to admit he was suitably impressed. She had his mother pegged, but she had now trailed off and was staring at him. After a minute he said, "Go on, I am listening."

The problem was Madison was not exactly sure where to go from there. She had strong feelings about the matter, but she could not quite put them into words. She hated when that happened. She stood there rubbing her palms together, trying to figure out what to say. "I think the answer lies in what happened that day between you and your brother. I think if you want to put this all to an end, you have to find the answers there."

"That is ridiculous. I am not going over that." He started to turn and walk away.

She grabbed him by the arm. "I think that is the problem. You keep running away from it. What happened?"

He snarled and jerked his arm free. "None of your damn business." He kept walking.

"Then go on. Keep walking, continue to damn your people to this life, or lack of life. Do you think it has escaped my notice that there are no children here? What happened to all the village children, Mathias? Is this what you want for you? Is this what you want for your people? Where are the children?"

Mathias grabbed the hair at the back of his neck, as he threw his head back and howled, "I do not know!"

"What do you mean, you do not know? What happened? Talk to me, please. I just want to help."

He rounded on her. "I do not know what happened to the village children! They were all gone when we all became like this! …" He held out his arms palms out to her. "… They all disappeared. There is no one in my kingdom under the age of sixteen. It is all part of the damn curse."

"What happened between you and your brother?" She hesitated, then she pressed the advantage. She stepped forward and placed both hands gently on his chest as she looked up at him pleadingly, she asked very gently, "What happened to Jared? He had just turned eighteen, had he not?"

Mathias looked down at her, his shoulders started shaking. He opened his mouth several times. "I got him killed. It was supposed be fun, like a game, just the two of us. It was only a pack of wolves. We were two skilled hunters. We should have been able to handle them, but I got him killed. I arrogantly thought the two of us could kill a pack of wolves. They were just animals and causing problems with the flocks. I mean, it was just a pack of wolves. I thought seven or eight, right. Try more like twenty or thirty. Jared was good, but he was not good enough. I got him killed. I should never have taken him out alone with me. I should have taken a couple of the hunters with us, but I thought it would be fun, just the two of us brothers, an overnight excursion. When I saw how many there were, I told him to get into the trees, but he did not listen." He pulled free, taking several steps back, holding his hands out in front of him palms up, staring at them as though there were something on them. "I still have nightmares about it. They tore him to pieces. I managed to kill them all and then I went down to get his body." His shoulders started shaking again as tears slid down his cheeks. "I would not let anybody see him like that. I found all of the pieces of him, and I wrapped them in my cloak, then I made a litter, and I brought him back here, then I buried him. I murdered my little brother. It is my fault." He dropped to his knees and buried his face in his hands.

Madison could feel tears sliding down her own cheeks. She crossed to him and wrapped her arms around his shoulders. He buried his face in her breast and sobbed uncontrollably. She frowned as she considered what she had heard. Maybe she was biased, but she did not think it sounded like Mathias was responsible at all. She had heard somewhere that curses only had power if you gave them power?

Maybe that was the problem, Mathias had been feeding it. "I know it is cruel to ask for details at a time like this, but you said you told him to get into the trees. Who was closer, you or him?"

He pulled free and wiped his face. He closed his eyes, forcing himself to relive that moment, recalling every detail.

*****

Mathias was walking towards the woods, Jared beside him. Neither one of them had spoken since they left the Castle, but Mathias could feel it coming. Jared clearly had something on his mind.

Jared demanded, "Why do you insist on provoking Mother?"

"Why does she insist on making her hatred for me so obvious?"

Jared sighed and shook his head. "You know Mother is difficult. I do not think she actually hates you, but I will agree she does not much like you, but you do not help the situation. Why are you being such an ass about getting married? Either take one of her suggestions or tell her you will choose your own damn bride, but I really think you are only doing this to get under her skin. I love you, big brother, but you are making my life difficult."

Mathias considered that for a long minute. "I refuse to have a marriage like Mother and Father. I want the woman in my bed to be happy to be there. I want to be happy she is there, but more importantly than any of that, I want her to love my children equally. Do not get me wrong, Jared, I do not begrudge you Mother's love, I just wish she would spread a little my way. Father did not love me less when you came along, and he loved you as much as he loved me."

Jared sighed and nodded. "I am sure the right woman is out there for you, Mathias." He started laughing. "The problem with you is …" he reached over and shoved his brother in the head, "… with that damned thick skull of yours, you will not even know her when you see her. By the time you get around to admitting that she is the one you want, she will be married to someone else with three or four children." Mathias growled, turned, and glared at him. Jared only laughed harder.

Mathias shoved his little brother in the shoulder, forcing him sideways then he shoved him again in the chest with both hands, knocking him on his ass. "Shut up, wise ass." Jared continued to laugh. All of a sudden Mathias' ears perked up. He held his hand up indicating his brother was to be silent. They both listened carefully. Mathias held his hand out to Jared and pulled into his feet. As he unslung his bow he whispered softly, "I can hear them moving ahead of us, about twenty yards that direction. Moving slowly." Mathias turned and headed to intercept the pack. Jared unsheathed his sword. Mathias shook his head. "No, that is not a good idea. Use your bow. You do not want them that close to you. Your sword should be a last resort."

Jared snorted, "I can handle it."

Mathias' concern was growing. He thought for sure the pack shifted in their direction. That did not make sense. If they had heard them, they should be heading in the opposite direction. He slowed his pace. Jared passed him. Mathias said quickly, "No, stay with me."

Jared did not listen and moved to engage the wolves, saying as he did, "Stop treating me like a child."

Mathias nocked an arrow as he said angrily, "Stop acting like one. Use your bow. You do not want them that close." A moment later the first one came into sight. Mathias let the arrow fly, burying it in the wolf's head. He immediately nocked another arrow, then he swallowed hard as he realized how many there were. He shouted quickly, "We cannot take them all on here on the ground, get to the trees! There are too many of them!" Mathias slung his bow over his shoulder as he headed for one of the trees. He was nearly there when one of the wolves jumped on his back. He felt its claws rake into his flesh. He hit the ground hard, scrambling, trying to get the wolf off of him. Then he felt it bite into his back several times. He screamed in pain. "Jared, get to the trees!" He rolled, drawing his dagger. The wolf charged him again. He stabbed him in the neck, got to his feet, grabbed his bow and slung it over his shoulder, then made a run for the trees. He jumped and grabbed a tree branch. It took him a moment to pull himself up. Jared was still on the ground, fighting them with his sword. They were swarming him. Mathias began loosing arrow after arrow, trying to get them off of Jared. He shouted angrily, "Get to the trees! I will clear the way." But it was too late, one of the wolves jumped, burying his teeth in Jared's throat taking him to the ground.

*****

Mathias screamed angrily, "Dammit Jared, why did not you listen to me?" He buried his face in his hands. "If only he would have listened, he would not be dead now."

Madison stared at him sobbing for another minute, then she realized she felt very dizzy, and her eyes were playing tricks on her. It appeared as though all the colors were running. As she stared a moment longer, she realized they were not running but becoming dust and they were blowing away. After another minute, Mathias's head completely disappeared, then his shoulders, then all of the colors were swirling together in a dust storm. She shut her eyes, convinced she was about to faint. When she opened them, everything was coming back into focus. She was relieved to discover she was standing against a wall. She pressed her hands into the cold stone as the dust began to form new shapes. She looked down at herself. Why had she not become dust, but remained solid the whole time? She thought to herself, *Why does this realm hate me?* Finally everything was solid again, but she was not outside the Castle.

They were now in Mathias's office. Mathias was standing, leaning on his desk, both palms pressed into the wood, his shoulders slumped, looking as though he needed it for support. His clothes were torn and covered in dried blood and dirt. His back was to the door and torn to pieces. He looked like he needed to be in the infirmary, not in his office. Rosemary was standing in the middle of the room looking confused. Louisa was standing in the doorway holding the door frame with one hand, her other hand was to her stomach. She, too, looked confused.

Rosemary recovered first. She shouted angrily, "No, you could not have! How did you break the curse?" She screamed in anguish, then she looked down. Too late, Madison realized she had a dagger attached to her belt. She grabbed it, brought it up to shoulder height and started for Mathias, who had just turned around. She was only able to take two steps when the dagger disintegrated in her hand.

A very familiar voice said, "I think, Rosemary, you have caused enough trouble for your son today. I think it is time he be free of you, once and for all." Rosemary seemed to be trying to move, but she seemed frozen. There was a swirl of dust next to her and Gretchen appeared. "I think my sisters and I will put you somewhere safe, where you cannot harm anyone again."

Mathias turned and stared. He pointed at the woman next to his mother. After minute he said, "You are not a member of my Castle. That is really odd, because I remember you. You have been here every day for the past hundred and whatever years, but you were not here before, but I thought you were. I do not understand. Why were you here?"

Gretchen inclined her head. "My sisters and I decided that someone needed to be here to oversee things until you found your way out of the curse. I volunteered. After all ..." she sighed and looked disgusted, "... I did teach Rosemary everything she knows. It was kind of my fault. So I have been here keeping an eye on things, but I was starting to get the idea you were never going to forgive yourself, not that you needed forgiving. It was not your fault, but you could not seem to admit that. You were determined to blame yourself, so I decided to enlist some aid." She placed her hand on Rosemary's shoulder. "But if you will excuse us, I need to take her away. I will be back later." She winked at Mathias. "Much later, after you have had time to settle in. I think you will need me, though I could be wrong." She and Rosemary disappeared in a swirl of dust.

Mathias felt dizzy and very confused. Everything seemed to be one massive blur, then he saw Louisa. She started forward and they embraced in the middle of the room. "Oh my God, I cannot tell you how much I have missed this." He hugged her tightly, refusing to let her go, caring nothing for the pain.

Madison raised an eyebrow and decided she really did not want to stay and watch. She was only a few feet from the door, and since no one had noticed her, and she was starting to think they might have even forgotten about her. She decided it was best if she just tiptoed out. Once outside of the office, she headed for the Castle's main entrance. To her surprise, every member of the Castle staff stared at her in surprise, but then they continued on about their work as though they had not recognized her. She headed for the Castle Gates. The guards, too, seemed to be going about their day's work. One of them demanded, "How did you get inside the Castle walls? Who are you?"

"No one. Not to worry, I am just leaving." She hurried through the Castle Gates, not wishing to be thrown in a cell until His Majesty had time for her. Something told her he was going to be very busy for some time. It was only when she reached the outskirts of the village that it occurred to her to look at the Castle. She turned around, it was a beautiful sight. All four towers were completely untouched, the grounds and the walls looked immaculate. Something told her only the people in that room actually remembered what had happened. She heard children playing. She looked to see. Watching for a moment, she smiled. Everything seemed to be back to normal. That was good. It made her happy. She turned back and analyzed her direction. She decided that after the story she had just heard, the trees did not sound very appealing. She headed for the river. When she arrived, she found some stones and sat and watched the river go by, wondering how close she was to where she had come into this realm.

XXI

Madison was enjoying watching the river drift by, it was very peaceful here. She liked it very much. She especially liked the fact that she was at least six feet away from the water. She pulled her skirt up to past her knees and removed her boots, then she rubbed her feet along the soft grass. It was a lovely. It made her feel very comfortable. The river seemed very slow and lazy. She had no idea how long she had been sitting there, when she asked herself, "I wonder if I am going to be allowed to stay here. I do not want to go home. I like it here." She laughed at herself. She sounded very snobby. "You know there's no reason for proper grammar anymore, I don't think I'll be staying." A hand grabbed her arm and yanked her to her feet. She stared up as Mathias' arms went around her.

He said angrily, "You really are out to break every rule today, are you not?"

She blinked as she continued to stare up at him. The voice was the same, but the face was definitely not. Even though she had seen him back in the office, it had been easy to think of him as a different person, especially as disheveled as he was, covered in dirt and blood. Now it was undeniable that he was in fact Mathias. As she studied him, he was again immaculately dressed and now appeared unharmed. She realized he was slightly older than his coronation painting and he had a beard. She was surprised that she found she thought he looked good that way. As she continued to stare into his steely gray eyes, she felt all warm and tingly and it took her a minute to find her voice. "I thought you and Louisa should be left alone to get reacquainted, and I figured since the curse was broken, my presence was no longer required."

He snorted. "Louisa would never let me hear the end of it if I let you slip through my fingers." He leaned forward to kiss her.

She looked away as she put her palm over his mouth. He pressed a kiss to her hand as she demanded, "And exactly what kind of relationship would you like to have with me, since clearly you and Louisa are intimately acquainted." Mathias could not help it, he roared with laughter. She gave him a little shove. "And what, Your Majesty, do you find so funny?"

"Louisa and I are not intimately acquainted."

She cut him off. "But back in your office you said you'd missed holding her in your arms."

Mathias laughed harder. "Yes, I did very much miss hugs from my great aunt. She is the only woman around the Castle who ever gave a damn about me." He tried to kiss her again.

She put both hands against his chest and pushed back. "That is impossible! Louisa's like what, thirty?"

He laughed and tapped the side of her head. "You still think like someone from Earth. Louisa is a witch. They age incredibly well. She is my grandfather's illegitimate older sister. I think she is probably like a hundred, maybe older. I never asked. It is kind of rude. She came to live in the Castle when I was about nine, when her husband died of old age. I think he was like ninety-five, and something tells me she was not thirty when she married him."

"But you do not call her Aunt Louisa."

"I cannot. As I said, she is my grandfather's illegitimate sister. It would be embarrassing to her to have our family connection known, then everyone would know what she was. Believe me, my life in the Castle got a lot easier when she came to live here. She and my father got on very well. She and my mother not so much. That never bothered me any. Now stop coming up with arguments and just kiss me. I have wanted to kiss you for so long." He leaned forward to kiss her, but she looked away. He pressed a kiss to her neck, then asked, "Now what?" He kissed her neck again.

"You didn't answer me about what kind of relationship we would have. You're the King and I'm a deformed peasant outsider."

He tightened his grip around her, pulling her against him, and snorted with amusement. "Your vocabulary has fallen dramatically, Louisa would be appalled. If you think I would settle for anything less than marriage, you have not learned anything about me, and I do not care what other people think. I may be a spoiled, rotten, arrogant brat, but I care very much about my family name and honor. All of my children will be born on the right side of the blanket, so will you marry me?"

Madison did not know what came over her. She felt tingly all over and her knees felt a little weak. It was not like her to go all gooey, she was usually a hard-core realist. Which was probably why it was on the tip of her tongue to say he could not possibly want to marry her, but she told herself, *For God's sakes, shut your mouth before you shoot yourself in the foot. Just kiss him.* She decided to be sensible and listen to her inner voice and kissed him.

He stood there holding her in his arms, kissing her for several minutes, then he pulled his mouth free. "And one more thing, if you are ever going to be so scandalous as to show your legs off by the stream again, you had better be making love to me, is that understood?"

She blushed deeply. "Perfectly, Your Majesty."

He grinned. "Good." Then he went back to kissing her.

Epilogue

Madison was in the sitting room, trying to draw Charles from memory. It was coming along rather nicely. She could not believe that the curse had now been broken for six weeks. She and Mathias had been married for five and everything seemed to be going very nicely. They still had many unanswered questions, but Gretchen said she would return. They just had to wait and see. She frowned. She wondered if Gretchen was even really her name.

"But of course, why would I give a false name? That would have been unnecessarily complicated. I mean, it is not like anyone knew who I was anyways."

Madison started and looked up. Gretchen was standing in the middle of the room. She gave a slight curtsy. "Good morning, Your Majesty. How are you doing? I must say, you look incredibly happy."

Madison smiled and got to her feet, dropping her sketchbook where she had just been sitting. "Well, I am glad I do not have to learn a new name for you. So nice to see you, Gretchen. Please sit down, I will ring for some tea." She crossed to the bell pull. When Margaret entered a minute later and curtsied, Madison asked, "Would you please inform His Majesty that we have company, and then bring in some tea and biscuits."

She curtsied. "Yes, Your Majesty, right away."

Madison returned to her seat. "I hope you are here to answer some lingering questions." She sat down, then she realized she had sat on her sketchbook, but it was not there. She looked up to see Gretchen thumbing through the sketches.

She held up one of Charles. "Do you think he is still angry at me about walking him off the cliff?"

Madison started laughing. "Something tells me immensely. That was you?"

She shrugged her shoulders, then held up her finger and twirled around. A little cloud of dust appeared and a moment later she was holding the dangling pendant. "Well, I did lead him astray with this. Sadly, the incantation does not work quite right. That is what I get for doing it in a hurry. Sorry about the rough landing, I will have to see if I can fix it. Just goes to show even the Coven are not infallible."

Mathias entered and raised an eyebrow. He crossed to his wife and sat down next to her. "Gretchen, to what do we owe this pleasure?"

"Well, Madison seemed to feel there were some unanswered questions, so I thought I would come and answer them. Maybe do a little favor I feel I owe Charles."

Mathias leaned forward. "There are definitely some lingering questions. Why does nobody else remember anything?"

She sighed. "Well, as you know, the coven cannot undo what others have done, but we can alter. The best we could do was to remove the children from the Castle and put them to sleep in our palace. We were also able to remove the kingdom from ordinary time, so that every day spent in your kingdom was only a second in the rest of the realm. So even though you have nearly a hundred and twenty years of memory, as does Louisa, and Madison has about ten weeks, in reality your kingdom was only separated for twelve hours, give or take. The children each had their own separate dreams. However, as to all the adults here, they were basically in a dream state, except you, Louisa, and then of course Madison, myself, and your mother. Let us not forget the troublemaker. And of course, like any dream, only a few minutes after they awoke they had no memory of it. Does that explain everything?"

"It was the Coven who put my mother in the painting, was it not?"

She nodded grimly. "Yes, we could not allow a woman such as that freedom to cause trouble."

Madison considered for a moment. "I guess that clears everything up, except why do you owe Charles?"

"Well, I did walk him off the cliff. I feel very guilty about that and even though time here has been frozen, time in your realm has not, and your brother has felt the weight of every day. I feel very bad about this, so I thought I might send you to say a proper goodbye."

Madison got to her feet and clasp her hands together. She said with excitement, "Really, I could go home and see Charles for a little while?"

Gretchen smiled at her. "As long as you like, and I promise you, the journey this time will be much smoother."

Mathias got to his feet. "Now wait a minute, I do not like the idea of her going back without me. What if they try to lock her up again?"

Gretchen nodded. "I was concerned about that, which is why whenever she is ready to return, or whenever the two of you are ready to return, you merely have to call my name three times and I will bring you home. But I figured you would want to see her realm. After all, it is only fair, but I think you are going to find it rather shocking."

He wrapped his arm around his wife's waist. "I do not care, she is not going without me."

Madison looked up at her husband. "I do not suppose you would let me have my jeans and T-shirt back for this?"

"Absolutely not, I will not allow my wife to appear in public in such scandalous garments."

She sighed. "Very well, where will we be arriving?"

Gretchen got to her feet putting down the sketchbook down and tapping it, she said, "By the way, I restored all of the sketches that somebody destroyed. I think now he might find them more amusing than offensive." Mathias frowned. She rolled her eyes and said, "Then again, maybe not, and in regards to where you will be arriving, I was hoping you would have a clear memory of where you wanted to go. As long as you can picture it in your mind, I can send you there."

Madison considered for a minute. "I can imagine his back patio very clearly, does that work?"

"Yes. Start focusing. Mathias, hold onto her. I can bring you back by yourself, but I cannot send you by yourself. Madison's mind is the doorway." Mathias tightened his grip around his wife's waist with his right arm as he gripped her left hand with his. Everything started swirling around them. They heard Gretchen say from far away, "Start walking forward."

They did as they were told. A moment later everything around them cleared. Mathias looked around. They were standing on a stone veranda with a strange looking pond. "What is that? It looks like a fountain, only much bigger."

"It is called a swimming pool. Let us just hope Charles or his wife are home. Oh God, that means Barbara, good times."

She crossed to the glass doors, relieved to see the blinds were open. That meant somebody was home. She knocked on the glass. A moment later she saw Charles come out of his office. He crossed quickly to the door and yanked it open. "Madison, how on earth did you get back? Are you all right?" He froze as he looked at the man standing behind his sister. He demanded, "Who the hell is that?"

Mathias wrinkled his face. "What is hell? That does not sound like a very nice way to greet a guest."

Madison replied, "Hell is the unpleasant place you go when you die."

"I see, we call it eternal damnation."

Madison could not help it, she said quickly, "Then this would be shorter." He snorted. "You know, there are times I really understand why they turned you into a werewolf."

He shrugged his shoulders. "I always assumed it was because my mother called me an animal and I had just been attacked by wolves, but you might be right."

Charles blinked, then he asked, "He's from the other world, isn't he?"

Mathias and Madison said simultaneously, "Realm, not world."

Barbara hearing a commotion came out of the kitchen. She stared in astonishment. "Madison, where have you been and what are you wearing? I mean, it's pretty and all, but you look like you just came from a Renaissance Festival."

Charles stepped back and gestured for them to enter. Madison smiled. "Thank you, I think."

Mathias raised an eyebrow. "What did she say?"

Madison sighed. "A Renaissance Festival is a festival that celebrates a period of time way in the past, what is called the Renaissance. People dress up and look like they were living at the time. It is weird, but people like it."

Barbara looked annoyed. "I don't need a definition of a Renaissance Festival, and who's your friend, and what language is he speaking."

Charles and Madison exchanged looks, then each turned to their respective partners and demanded, "What?"

Charles demanded of Barbara, "You can't understand him?"

Madison demanded of Mathias, "You did not understand her?"

Barbara replied, "You can?"

Mathias said, "If I would have understood her, I would not have asked you what I did."

Everyone started speaking at once. Mathias put two fingers in his mouth and whistled loudly. They all stopped speaking and turned to face him. He nodded and said, "Clearly, the two of you traveling to my realm allowed me to understand you and you to understand me, but since she has not traveled to my realm, we cannot understand each other. It probably has something to do with the magic of my realm and the lack of magic in this realm. Perhaps at a later time we can discuss this with Gretchen, and perhaps we can arrange a visit for your family to my realm."

Madison nodded and replied, "Oh that makes perfect sense. That is going to complicate things." She turned to her brother. "Please tell me you finally told her everything."

He frowned. "I did, but I don't think she really believed me."

Barbara crossed her arms over her chest and said, "Would someone please explain to me what is going on?"

Charles replied quickly, "Remember the other world I told you about, the one I traveled to and came back, and you thought I was drunk? Well, he's from the other world."

Mathias and Madison said simultaneously, "Realm."

"Sorry, he's from the other realm. Apparently you can't understand him and he can't understand you."

"So everything you told me was real? Oh wow! Who is he?"

Charles replied, "I think we were just getting to that, but how are we going to help them to communicate?"

Madison considered for a moment. "I have got it. If Barbara's speaking, you repeat everything she says, then Mathias will understand it. If Mathias is speaking, I will repeat everything he says, and since they both understand you and I, we are golden. There, I will quickly catch Mathias up on the conversation, you can catch Barbara up."

When this was done, Mathias said, "She is wearing that and she questions your garments? I cannot believe he permits his wife to wear such a thing outside of her bedchamber."

Madison and Charles both looked Barbara up and down. She was wearing a knee length straight skirt and a silk tank top. After moment Barbara demanded, "What?"

They both said simultaneously, "Nothing."

Charles tentatively extended his hand to Mathias. "Perhaps we should perform introductions. I'm Charles Brewster and this is my wife, Barbara."

He shook his hand. "Yes, we have met before, though we did not exchange names. I am King Mathias of Glacier Guard."

Charles stared at him for a moment, then asked, "Wait a minute, you were the angry man in the Throne Room? And you're criticizing how I greet guests?"

"Yes, you were trespassing and bleeding on my chair, of course, I was going to be angry. It is not my fault you came through the back door and did not ring the bell, so yes, I was angry."

Madison started laughing. "He was having a little bit of an attitude problem. His Castle was falling down around his ears."

"So hopefully His Majesty is here to return my sister, and then he's going to go away?"

Mathias crossed his arms over his chest. "I will go away, but she goes with me."

"Now wait a minute!"

Madison sighed. "Charles, my husband. Husband, my brother. Can y'all please be nice to each other, if for nothing else for me?"

Mathias snorted. "What did Louisa tell you about the word 'y'all'?"

Barbara raised an eyebrow. "You married him? Way to go!"

Charles stared at his wife and said, "Really, Barbara?"

She shrugged her shoulders. "Oh come on, he's gorgeous, like something out of a romance novel."

Madison took a deep breath and let it out slowly, then she stepped on her husband's foot. He smiled. "Can the two of you please choose to get along?"

Mathias nodded. "Better."

Charles turned and demanded of his sister, "Did you want to marry him?"

She wrapped her arms around Mathias's waist and smiled from ear to ear. "Most definitely. He can be a bit of a shit, but I like him anyways. Oh, that reminds me, I am supposed to tell you Gretchen's sorry about walking you off a cliff, but it was necessary, and she apologizes for the very rough landing. That is what happens when you have to make enchanted magic items on the fly.

They sometimes have problems." She let go of Mathias and hugged her brother. "I cannot tell you how much I have missed you."

Charles held her for a long time, then he pulled free, gripped her face with both hands and kissed her on the forehead. "Come on in, both of you. Sit down, tell us everything. I want to hear all about your life."

The End

Made in the USA
Middletown, DE
16 November 2024